Fracture
Point

Peter
Apps

AUP UK
Terrestrial And Universal
Publications

Published by TAUP UK

TAUP UK
Sheerness
Kent

enquiries@taup.uk

Preface

It's an old adage but it's still true that reporters never let the facts get in the way of a good story. It is also true of most authors to a greater or lesser extent so there is always a risk that a serious point in a story is overlooked because too much disbelief has been suspended.

Fracture Point describes an event that hopefully will not happen but solar flares are frequently observed. Whether they are a threat is a matter of science fact not science fiction but a serious discussion of those facts is probably inappropriate here.

However, the questions raised by this tale are valid and it would be nice to know what contingency plans are in place to deal with such a disaster. Sadly though, I imagine that official reaction is that solar flares have never been a serious problem in the past so it is unlikely that they would be a threat in the future.

My reasons for believing that such a disaster is possible are contained in *Appendix A* at the back of this collection. Add in stories of riots during power cuts and the effects of shock then the events depicted become even more plausible

If you are a scientist or a politician in the know then please contact me and tell me that I've got it all wrong. It would be nice to delete this prologue and *Appendix 'A'* from future editions leaving Fracture Point as a simple fictional story.

You may also be interested in the BBC transcript from the 1970s adapted for use in this story. I have reproduced it in *Appendix 'B'* as it offers an insight to official government thinking and its ability to cope with a catastrophic breakdown of society.

Day 1

"Shit." David swore angrily as he watched the police car do a hurried U-turn to follow him.

Still, he could still have some fun and maybe he would get lucky. As he tore his eyes from the rear view mirror, he pressed his foot down on the accelerator. If he could get back to the estate he could abandon the car and lose himself in the warren of alleyways, walkways and paths that surrounded the high rise flats. He knew that the odds were against him but the longer he held the police at bay the better he felt about himself. He needed to prove that he was stronger and cleverer than them.

In other circumstances he could be making a name for himself in motor racing. He had good instincts, reading the road ahead and reacting calmly but instantly to any situation that developed. He had grown up in a stereotypically bad family, a father who vanished when he was five and a drug addicted mother. There was also an assortment of uncles, aunts and cousins who were none too bright and spent much of their time in prison.

As it was, he had done well to steer clear of drug addiction and alcohol dependency. He had even succeeded in getting a few school certificates. Neither did he get caught as often as he should for a string of petty thefts and motoring offences.

He was active enough to be fit and healthy with naturally boyish good looks. He was bright and friendly enough so that on occasions when they were both *off duty* he could sit and have a cup of coffee with the police he knew best; the ones who arrested him the most often.

He should have got to Margate in time for a night in the pubs and night clubs before the car had even been reported missing. Holding out against the pressures to conform had made him a few enemies. At night if he was out then, as those around him got drunker, he became more of a target for their anger and frustration so he found himself struggling to avoid a fight, which is why he chose Margate. Of the people who could see beyond their next fix, few could see beyond the familiar bricks and mortar of London and of those few who could see further, most would choose more fashionable venues. He would have been among strangers not wanting to cause him trouble but now, he was likely to be spending the night in the cells. He was not sure how he had been spotted so quickly. The cop had probably recognised him rather than the car and it was just bad luck.

He swore again more profusely and forcefully when he saw the helicopter circling the estate. He had been recognised and his gentle change of direction had been correctly interpreted. It was a nice car and he liked driving it so he was not ready to give up.

He needed to get close to a block of flats. If he could get inside so that the police could not see him for a few moments then he could turn and look as if he was leaving claiming that he had been visiting someone. When the police arrived he would still be stopped but he would have something. It might not be enough to get away but even if it made the police work harder, it would be something.

He glanced upwards and the helicopter was still there. He swore again. The traffic lights were out. If he needed to, he could mount the pavement to slip past the lights but the traffic had already piled up enough to make that manoeuvre tricky. The police car had dropped back when the helicopter had taken over so it was struggling with the traffic as well, though with its horns and sirens it was making more headway than David.

He still hesitated but there were not many pedestrians so he edged out of the line of traffic onto the pavement and round the corner into the side road he was trying for. He breathed a sigh of relief as the helicopter veered off and disappeared over the roof tops.

Maybe they've been called away on a more urgent task, he thought. It was odd because the police car still had not made it round the corner. It occurred to him that the helicopter had developed engine trouble or something but he did not worry about it for long, he had a chance to escape.

He took a sharp left followed by a sharp right then pulled into a car park. Another sharp turn and he was hidden behind the houses. He was out of the car in a flash, dashing through an alleyway before stopping, making himself relax, then sauntering off as if he did not have a care in the world. As he walked, he figured out the pub that he could have been visiting, which put him on his way home if he was questioned.

David knew that he had been lucky and that the police had

messed up in some way. The less he hurried the more innocent he looked, so he was more than willing to stop when an elderly man called out to him.

"Excuse me. Has there been a power cut?"

"I've no idea mate." David called back, "The traffic lights are out but you got a fuse blown or something?"

"I don't know." the man replied, "The box is in the cupboard under the stairs and I can't see as well I used to. I don't suppose you could take a look, could you?"

Perfect. He could get off the street and probably drag things out for an hour or so. The old man let him in and showed him to the cupboard. The fuse box was old with the old fashioned wire type fuses. David made a show of turning the power off then pulling each fuse out in turn to study it.

"We've got gas." the old man said, "My wife can boil a saucepan of water for a cup of tea if you'd like one?"

"Yes please." David replied, beginning to feel really safe. He was a little puzzled because all the fuses were intact. Even if one had blown, the others should have been working.

"I think it must be a power cut." David said, "You seem to be fine. Maybe you should ring the electricity company and find out how long it'll be off."

"Would you do it for us please?" the old man asked, "I get so confused when they say press one for this, two for that and so on."

David nodded and picked up the phone almost dropping it as a deafening hiss assaulted his ear. He was a little concerned now. He knew that phones did not fail because of power cuts and two incidents were a bit of a coincidence. He took his mobile out of his pocket and looked at it. The signal bars were blank and 'No Service' was printed across the screen.

Taking a deep breath, knowing that he was blowing his cover, he dialled the emergency number. There was no response, just the no service message on the screen. The 999 call should have worked even if his other calls were blocked for some reason.

"Have you got a battery radio?" he asked.

"I've got one down the shed." the old man replied, "Shall I get it?"

"Yeah." David nodded. The lack of police coordination, the electricity, land line phone and now the mobile was too much of a coincidence. He was more scared now but the first rule of street life was, never show fear. The old man's wife looked worried, but seemed reassured that he was there.

The radio blared out the same hiss as the phone but as he listened he was sure that it was fading. The couple were looking at him, waiting.

"I reckon it's sun spots or something." he said, not knowing what he was talking about. He had heard them blamed for bad TV reception so it was as good a guess as any, "How about that cup of tea? Would you like me to stay for a while until they get it sorted?"

He was still thinking in terms of staying low for a while but the old couple grinned happily and the wife hurried off to make the drink.

"I'm Tom, by the way." the old man said trying to make conversation, "My wife's called Gladys. Thank you so much for helping like this."

Although Tom was well into his seventies he could pass for fifty. He was a big man, almost two metres but with a body proportionally large. Nowadays he had trouble seeing close up and arthritis made him clumsy when handling small or delicate objects. He would happily spend all day digging his garden, but a job like the fuse box left him lost and frustrated, feeling his age.

"I'm David." he replied, "It's no problem."

He was interrupted by someone knocking on the door, briefly scared that the police could have found him. David could hear the tone of the conversation at the door so that, by the time that Tom showed the caller into the living room he was back to his normal cheerful self.

"We're fine." Tom was saying, "David's looking after us. He reckons it's sun spots and we'll have to wait while it's sorted. This is Chloe."

"I hope it's quick." Chloe exclaimed, "I've got to collect Emma and Oliver from school then start their dinner. How long will the food last in the freezer?"

Everyone looked at David. He was eighteen, the youngest one there and everyone seemed to be turning to him.

"I don't know." David admitted, "Do you have a gas cooker?"

"No! I'm all electric."

"How about bringing some food here so that Gladys can cook

4

it." David suggested, "Use it up first and stockpile as much tinned food as possible."

"Why?" Tom asked, "How long do you expect it to last?"

"Again, I don't know." David answered, "Don't you think that we should play safe?"

"I don't have to go for an hour or so." Chloe said, "We'll see if it's back on then."

"How far away is the school?" David asked.

"Oh it's only ten minutes." Chloe replied, "The real problem's trying to find somewhere to park."

"The High Street traffic lights are out." David said, "It was already piling up when I came through. It'll be chaos now even if the power comes back on. I suggest you walk."

Chloe stared at him before nodding her head. She handed Tom her front door key, telling him to collect what they needed and headed off. David accompanied Tom to Chloe's house to collect the food.

"You're more worried than you say." Tom said, "What's really happening?"

"I keep saying that I don't know." David replied, "I've got a bad feeling about it all. I hope I'm wrong but…"

He tailed off not sure what he was worried about. Tom nodded in understanding.

"You'd better get home, lad," he said, "your folks will need you and I'm grateful for what you've done."

"Mum's got one of her tricks coming over." David said bitterly, "I'll stay out-of-the-way for now. She'll want to find a dealer after. If the lights don't come back on tonight, she'll just want me to sit there and tell her it'll be all right until she starts getting strung out again. Then she'll want me to find her dealer again. I'd rather be in a place where I can do something."

"You've got a good head on you, lad." Tom said, "Let's get this meal sorted and Gladys will get the spare room ready for you. You can stay as long as you like."

While Tom raided the freezer, David put his petty thief skills to good use and quickly searched the house. Ignoring his usual plunder he looked for batteries, lanterns, candles and anything else that might prove useful. Tom looked at him quizzically.

David returned his stare a bit sheepishly, "Tell her what I've done if you like. If she comes back here tonight she can bring it all with her but it might be safer to stay in one place after dark."

Tom nodded his understanding, "I'll talk to the women and explain. You're thinking on your feet, you're worried and you could be right."

Chloe was badly shaken when she returned. Traffic was at a standstill. Shops were closed and people were just milling around. She saw frightened passengers being led out of an underground station.

The school had been an oasis of calm as teachers tried to comfort their students but it was not easy. She was grateful that she had taken David's advice to walk, arriving early and one of the few parents to make it.

Emma was eleven and Oliver thirteen, well able to walk home on their own. However, if the school sent children off who were usually collected, then there could be problems if the parents arrived to pick them up. Other parents would not know that the school was closing early and might not appreciate their kids being let loose on the streets especially as things were at the moment.

Chloe had collected her children along with eleven others that she knew. Eight had been dropped off without problems while another three had stuck notes through their doors explaining that Chloe was looking after them and where they could be collected.

Like David, they were too old to show their fear but they were obviously as shaken as Chloe. They sat quietly waiting for the grown ups to put everything right. They felt better when Gladys offered them tea and sandwiches followed by biscuits and sweets. Gladys was an old fashioned kindly soul. Whatever else was going on, she had guests and they would be properly looked after.

As they were finishing, there was a knock at the door. Tom answered it bringing a stranger through. One of the visiting girls rushed over to hug and greet him.

"Thanks for looking after Carol." Brian Masters said.

"It's been a pleasure." Gladys replied, "Would you like a cup of tea?"

"No thanks." Brian replied, "I want to be home for when Debs gets in. The journey from Colchester must be horrific."

David started to say something but stopped. Only Tom noticed.

"Go on say it." he almost snapped.

"It's just my opinion," David said cautiously, "but I don't think your wife stands a chance of getting from Colchester, tonight."

He was less confident than usual, beginning to really worry about what was happening.

"Nonsense." Chloe snapped, "You keep trying to make a drama out of this power cut. They'll run a shuttle service using diesels or something. The motorways will be clear. They'll put on coaches."

"Maybe." David conceded, "How big is this power cut? Why are the phones and mobiles out? How do they organise shuttles without phones or computers?"

"Dad works in the city." one of the boys said, "Mum teaches in a school in Epping. I hope they're OK. Maybe Jake and me should go home and wait for them."

"No." David said firmly, "We've left a note to say where you are. You stay here."

"You can't tell us what to do." the boy said petulantly, "We're going."

"I don't argue with little kids like you." David said, the menace obvious in his voice, "You try to leave and I'll break your fucking legs."

Night 1

Chloe and Gladys looked shocked and all the children obviously even more scared.

"That's a bit harsh." Tom said mildly

"Sorry." David said, "We don't need kids playing up."

He took a deep breath trying to calm down.

"It's getting dark now." he explained, "There's no street lights. I wouldn't want to cross the street let alone find my way to another one."

"We could take a torch." the boy persisted, "Besides, it's not that dark. What's that funny light in the sky?"

For a moment they were distracted as they crowded outside to look at the sky. Instead of being black it was lit by dancing shimmering lights filling the sky from horizon to horizon. It was bright enough to read by.

"It's the Aurora Borealis." Oliver interjected proudly "They're the Northern Lights."

He paused uncertainly, "At, least that's what they look like but you don't see them in England."

"Whatever." David retorted, "Even if you do get home what happens when some guy like me decides he needs your stuff more than you?"

The boy stood still, unsure what to do.

"What's your name, son?" Tom asked.

"Rory." the boy replied.

"Well listen Rory." Tom said gently, "We don't know how bad things are going to get yet and David is saying that we need to work together. He shouldn't have threatened you but he's been right so far and it may be safer to do as he says."

In a way Rory was relieved, glad to hear that someone was in control.

"It's coming up to the hour." Gladys said, "See if you can find a news summary."

Tom nodded and turned on the radio. There was still a lot of crackle and hiss but through the noise they heard someone speaking. It was difficult to understand what was being said, reception was so bad. Sometimes the message was completely unintelligible but it was repeated several times and gradually they pieced the announcement together.

This is an Emergency Broadcasting Service Announcement. It is being broadcast on all operational public and commercial radio channels.

A solar flare has struck the Earth. Communications have been severely disrupted. The number of casualties and the extent of the damage are not yet known. We shall bring you further information as soon as possible. Meanwhile, stay tuned to this wavelength, stay calm and stay in your own homes.

The immediate danger has passed. There is no radiation hazard. The food chain is unharmed. The only known damage has been to power cables and telecommunications. Work has already begun to restore these services. Some radio communications have already been re-established.

Remember there is nothing to be gained by trying to get away. By leaving your homes you could be exposing yourselves to greater danger. If you leave, you may find yourself without food, without water, without accommodation and without protection.

If mains water is available, this can be used for fire-fighting. You should also refill all your containers for drinking water after the fires have been put out, because the mains water supply may not be available for very long.

Water must not be used for flushing lavatories: until you are told that lavatories may be used again, other toilet arrangements must be made. Use your water only for essential drinking and cooking purposes. Water means life. Don't waste it.

Make your food stocks last: ration your supply, because it may have to last for fourteen days or more. If you have fresh food in the house, use this first to avoid wasting it: food in tins will keep.

Here are the main points again: Stay in your own homes. Make sure that the gas and all fuel supplies are turned off and that all fires are extinguished. Water must be rationed, and used only for essential drinking and cooking purposes. It must not be used for flushing lavatories. Ration your food supply: it may have to last for fourteen days or more.

We shall repeat this broadcast in an hour's time. Stay tuned to this wavelength, but switch your radios off now to save your batteries until we come on the air again. That is the end of this broadcast.

Everyone looked at David.

"What's a solar flare?" Rory asked.

"I don't know." David replied.

"It's a burst of energy from the sun." Oliver piped up, "It's probably knocked out all the satellites and spiked the power cables."

"What do you mean, spiked?" Tom asked.

"It induces massive voltage spikes in any cable running for long distances. The spike can blow electronic equipment."

"It didn't sound so bad." Brian said, "They'll get London fixed up first so I'm taking Carol home. We can be there when Debs arrives. Thanks for your help."

"Brian's right." Gladys said, "We'll probably get the power back tomorrow."

"How are they going to order the parts?" David asked, "How will they arrange transport? How are they going to direct engineers to the right places to check the damage in the first place?"

"I don't know." Gladys replied, "The way they usually do, I suppose."

"Without computers, the Internet or phones?" David asked again, "The police helicopter couldn't even talk to a car directly below it, this afternoon."

"How do you know?" Chloe asked.

"Because they were chasing me and I only got away because it all went wrong."

"Why were they chasing you?" Chloe spoke angrily with a hint of disgust in her voice, "I don't think that we should be harbouring a criminal. Maybe you should go."

"I told you." David said bluntly, "No one goes anywhere in the dark. Tomorrow, I'm getting out of London. If anyone wants to come with me, you're welcome."

"The radio said that we should stay in our homes." Gladys said, "We should do as we're told and not make it harder on the authorities."

"Take a look out of the upstairs windows. How many fires can you already see?" David asked, "Listen and you can hear screams. I'm sure I've heard gunshots. My guess is that the shopping centres and the pubs are getting it tonight. I'm gonna do it the way the police do their raids. Leave at dawn when everyone is at their lowest, nick a bike and head for open country."

"Then what?" Chloe asked, still hostile.

"I don't know." David said, "I say that a lot don't I? It's true though and it's also the truth that nobody else does either."

"Yes they do." Chloe snapped, "The news announcement said they did and it had good advice. They know what they're doing."

"OK!" David sneered scornfully, "Maybe in a nice little road like this you can dig a hole in the lawn to shit into and maybe there's enough food to last us a fortnight. What about the people in those blocks of flats. Are they going to take a dump over the balcony? Most of them are out of work, how much food can they afford to stock up on? Even if you've got cash, who's going to serve you if the tills are dead? We ought to see how many of these houses are empty and gather up all the tinned stuff but if we stay put, how long before some gang is desperate enough to do it to us?"

"Must you be so crude?" Chloe asked testily, "Especially in front of children and I don't suppose that Tom and Gladys appreciate such language in their house."

David rolled up his eyes in despair.

"David may be blunt." Tom said, "I don't think now is the time to worry about it."

They were interrupted by a loud pounding on the front door.

"It's me, Ray March." a voice called out, "Is anyone in there?"

"Just a moment." Tom called in reply then in a normal voice, "Come with me, please David. The man's a bloody busybody and won't take no for an answer."

I hope it's not the Ray March at the Job Centre, David thought to himself, *He hates my guts.*

"Hi Tom." Ray said as the door opened, "We're getting a Neighbourhood Watch organised. I'm gathering up all the torches and batteries I can. I'll just pop in for a few minutes and tell you what we need."

"No way!" David exclaimed.

Ray frowned angrily as he recognised David.

"You'd better be on your way, Robson." he snapped, "We don't want your sort round here."

"David has been helping us." Tom said, "I'd like him to stay."

"We can't afford anyone from that estate hanging around." Ray said, still angry, "They've already looted the Belle and Lion then set fire to it. They're too drunk to do much for now but we've got to get ready. Now we need torches and weapons. Let's see what you've got."

"Use car headlights. There's plenty." David said, "If you park them side by side across the road you'll have a road block and lighting to see what's coming."

Ray was silent as he considered the idea until it occurred to him that he should not be taking advice from a layabout and a crook.

"We don't have enough and we don't need you to tell us what to do." he snapped, "Just get back to where you belong or I'll fetch a couple of friends to help you on your way."

"David is my guest and he'll leave when he's ready." Tom snapped back, equally angry, "According to Chloe the roads are blocked. I bet there's plenty of abandoned ones you could use."

The community where Tom lived had been built in the nineteenth century to accommodate the growing number of skilled artisans that a city of the time needed. As times changed so the area deteriorated and the houses became cheaper and shabbier. It was just far enough away from the centre of London to escape the worst of the blitz and then in the eighties and nineties it underwent a change as a place for up and coming city types to live.

Built near where the river Thames bends, it backs on to the river on two sides. On the third side was a creek. At least it probably started out as a creek but boat builders and warehouses lined the sides so that now, it looked more like a dock basin than a creek.

Nowadays, the river's edge catered for tourists more than river trade. A wide pedestrian path followed the river with pubs, cafés and parks to entertain the visitors. The inlet was still called the Creek but instead of barges and tugs it catered for pleasure craft, river-buses and house boats.

David had dumped the stolen car in a car park along the fourth edge and ducked inwards towards the centre of the community. He could have claimed to be heading home from one of the large anonymous tourist pubs where no one would remember whether he had been there or not.

Since the roads in the little community only led to the river, they were quiet. No one had turned into them trying to avoid the horrendous jams that the loss of all traffic lights in the city had caused.

If they had bothered to listen to David, then the residents could have defended their community quite well. Most of the houses were deserted. Ray would have described, them as decent hard working folk who were at work when the flare had struck, not loafing around on benefits.

Ray was lucky in that he worked in a local office but the further away anyone worked the less likely they were to get home. If Ray had been more imaginative he would have broken into the empty homes to secure as much food as possible, arranging for the fresh to be eaten first, leaving the preserved food to be stored. Even if a trickle of residents had returned, then they would hardly complain if, instead of being confronted with a freezer full of rotten food, they were offered supplies from the communal stock. Neither would they complain if the containers carefully stored in their cupboards had been pilfered and carried a ration of water for them but Ray was also a civil servant.

The law said you do not break into other people's property so he was incapable of doing so. He had heard the emergency broadcast and was used to handling people. His job did not allow him to be a bully but he was sure that David was not interested in finding a job, so he could cajole, harass and generally find ways to prove that he was in control.

He saw himself now as the senior government official present. He could use the emergency broadcast as an excuse to meddle by claiming that he was saving water, rationing food and protecting the community. No one, not even David knew what was really happening and most people, including Ray would trust the government, following its instructions. By contrast David was not so inclined to trust the authorities, especially someone like Ray March and David was intelligent enough to see that the situation was bad.

Even in the glow of the Northern lights, they could see isolated flames and fires in the distance. They had no idea whether they were made by frightened inhabitants trying to keep warm, trying to see what was going on or whether they were rioting looters burning everything they found.

Tom was far too calm and collected for Ray's liking. He had resisted Ray's efforts to take over and that was the Robson boy's fault but he knew that he would not be able to tackle them alone.

"I'll be back." he muttered as he strode away.

"I think I've heard that line before." Tom laughed as they closed the door.

"I think David's right about leaving. We should all leave." he continued when they returned to the living room, "But I'm not cycling. I'm going by boat."

David and the others stared at him.

"They've started to lay up the tourist boats for the winter. There's a couple in the Creek already. We could gather up all the supplies we could find, head out of the city and moor somewhere in the middle of nowhere until we find out what's happening."

"That's impossible." Chloe said, "What about my husband? What's he going to do when he gets back from his trip and we're gone. What about the boy's parents? You could get arrested for kidnapping."

"I don't know much about this survival shit." David said, "But it seems to me that our first job is to stay alive. I don't think we can do that here."

"We should wait for our families." Chloe persisted, "Tom, what about your son and his family. They'll be worried about you if you go gallivanting off."

There were tears in Tom's eyes as he replied, "They live near Guildford now. Graham works in Leatherhead, the girls go to school in Guildford and Emma works in Sunbury. If the roads are as bad as you say, they'll be lucky to find each other, let alone make it here."

"It might have been just a local jam." Chloe persisted, "You know what the local Council is like. Maybe it's just bad round here."

"All the traffic lights are computer controlled." Oliver said, "It won't be just here."

"You don't know for sure." Chloe replied desperately, "What have I said about you interrupting"

"It sounds as if he's our scientific expert." David said with a grin, "What do you think we should do?"

"You're scared of burglars if we stay here, aren't you?" Oliver asked.

"No, I'm thinking of looters getting desperate for food."

"That's what I meant but Mum says I shouldn't exaggerate." Oliver agreed, "You're thinking of those riots some time back."

David nodded.

"Let's listen to the news again and see if things are improving." Gladys suggested, "It's nearly time for the next one."

The same announcement was read out again, except that at the end the newsreader added,

Please stand by for some additional information.

If you are trapped in a town or city, unable to get home, please make your way to the nearest park or open space. Operations will begin at first light to drop food and supplies. Be patient and stay calm. Supplies may not arrive until late afternoon.

A State of Emergency has been declared. The police and armed forces have been authorised to use armed force to maintain law and order. Looters and anyone threatening supply distribution centres may be fired upon without prior warning.

That is the end of this broadcast.

"That doesn't sound very encouraging." Gladys said, "Maybe we should leave London after all."

"Yes but you heard." Chloe said, "They're organising food distribution and getting things under control. Mr. March will see that there's no trouble round here. We should stay."

"It makes sense." Gladys agreed then sounding exasperated, "Oh! I don't know what we should do."

"Why don't we pack as if we were going." Oliver said, "Then see what things are like when we're ready."

"Be quiet, Oliver." Chloe snapped, "You don't know what you're talking about."

"I think he does." Gladys said, "It wouldn't hurt to be ready. Just in case."

She looked at David, "Are we going together?"

"I don't know anything about boats." David said, "What about supplies for us all? I was planning to go alone and grab what I needed. I can't see you lot breaking the law."

"I worked on the river all my life." Tom said, "I started off on tugs docking ships in the Pool of London and finished up giving tourist commentaries. There's fuel, water and food if you know where to look. Some of it's more accessible by water than by road unless you've got motor transport and that's gridlocked so we should get to some of it first."

"And stealing it?" David asked.

"Typical." Chloe snapped, "We'll all end up in gaol or shot as looters. I still say that we stay put and work with Mr. March. He really does know what he's doing."

"My father had a way of describing people like him," Tom said, "dustman by day, managing director by night. He joins committees and voluntary organisations just to make himself look good. This could be his chance to really lord it over everyone. You know him David. What do you think?"

"He's a dickhead." David replied. David could be polite and well spoken but Chloe was riling him. He enjoyed seeing the look on her face whenever he swore, "He's got himself in charge and he's going to make sure everyone knows it."

"Let's get ready to go and see what's happening then." Tom said, "If things are still getting worse, then we should go. If law and order is breaking down then it's every man for himself."

"Will Mum and Dad be all right?" Jake asked suddenly in a tearful voice, "I'm scared."

"We all are." David replied as gently as he could, "You got all that email and stuff?"

"Yeah. I've got a laptop."

"We'll see if we can get to your place and pick it up along with your mobile phone chargers and everything." David said, "As soon as things start working again, you'll be able to find them. Until then, we have to stay as safe as possible."

"You said that we should stay together." Chloe exclaimed, "Now you want to go gallivanting off."

David angrily turned to her then glanced across to Gladys. For some reason Gladys made him nervous. She was content to let others do the talking but David felt that she appraised everything that was done. He did not want to find out what could happen if he fell too far below her standards.

He kept his temper, "Whatever we do, we need to get organised. Jake and Rory just wanted to go rushing off. I'm saying that I take them and then we all come back here. I'll take Ollie and Emma so that it's all done in one go."

"His name is Oliver." Chloe snapped, "He's not some street kid. We have standards."

"So what's your surname, Twist?" David asked angrily.

"That's enough, both of you." Gladys interrupted. She was not raising her voice but it had a harsh edge to it, "You've heard what it's

16

like outside. Even if the electricity comes back on now it'll be days before everything's back to normal. David, take the children to fetch their things. Jake, Rory, you do as David tells you. Chloe, this meat will last longer if it's cooked. Let's see how much we can do."

Oliver smiled to himself. He loved his mother but she still treated him as if he was five. He liked the way that David stood up to her.

"Jake, Rory, if your parents are back then you can stay with them." David said. He glanced at Gladys who nodded, "But it might be an idea if they came back here and brought as much stuff as they can."

"What happens if they don't get back?" Rory asked.

"Then you'll stay with us and we'll keep each other safe." David replied.

"And we'll be able to tell them when the Internet comes back on." Jake added for him.

David nodded. Even Chloe looked happier as the children considered their phones and computers. Tom went with them when David took the children to fetch their things. As they followed the children Tom spoke quietly to David, "You think it's a waste of time worrying about phones and things, don't you?"

David nodded, "I got off a lot because the computers often fouled-up. It was worth trying to twist the police up a bit. The more they used the things the more they were likely to make a mistake. This is one big foul-up."

Tom nodded, "It could be worldwide and that means we won't be getting help. Ever heard of a fracture-point."

David nodded, "It's when a bit of metal gets bent so far, it just snaps. You can't straighten it again."

"Do you think society's reached that point?" Tom asked.

David stared at Tom, not wanting to answer. Oliver had dropped back, listening to the adults.

"Yes I do." he said finally, "I should try to get mum but she wouldn't even visit Uncle Jack when he was in Maidstone Prison. You and the women are talking about leaving London but you won't though, will you? You don't really believe me, do you?"

"I do." Oliver said, "What's going to happen to us?"

"Good question." Tom said, "You're wrong about Gladys though, she's listening to you, and so am I. If we do go, she'll make

17

sure all the beds are made, the washing up's done, so that it's ready for us when we get back. A couple of years ago we went to stay with her brother in Australia for three months. She took to the life as if she'd been born there; barbecue on the beach for Christmas dinner and everything. The only thing she wanted was the house keys on her bedside cabinet where she could see them."

David and Oliver laughed.

"OK but taking a boat and hiding out on the river?" David asked.

Tom thought for a while, "I'm thinking we'll be safer moored in the middle of the creek than on land and that we can protect the children better. If we're careful, it won't be more than a couple of broken locks. They'll be more interested in looters and the like. If the news gets better, then we won't even have to do that. If it gets worse, then we should be ready."

The conversation ended as they reached Jake and Rory's house. The note Chloe had left was still on the table. Tom added to the note saying that he would look after the children for a few days if necessary but he would borrow some food and supplies in case the shops stayed closed.

Without the usual traffic noise and general hubbub of a busy city, London was eerily quiet. The only noises were shouts and screams in the distance. They sounded loud and close by but as Tom pointed out sound could travel a lot further. They heard the sound of breaking glass. It sounded nearby, possibly in the next street, but they did not see anything.

David was worried about showing a light at the front of the house that could attract attention so they stayed sitting in Gladys and Tom's living room. There was enough light from the Northern Lights to see. The males in the group went out into the garden and urinated against the garden fence when they needed to while the females still used the toilet. None of them were ready to disappear into the garden with a spade.

They lit the gas fire. Although they were nice and warm and it gave off a cheerful glow, Gladys was worried. She was sure that the flames were lower and became even lower during the evening. It might be because more people were turning to gas heating to replace electrical heaters but she wondered how long the gas supply could last without electricity.

Apart from that one expedition, none of them wanted to drift too far away from the others, not even to go upstairs to bed. In a normal blackout, they could listen to the radio, confident that the power would be back on soon and not even Tom or Gladys were used to both electricity and the phones being off. Gladys in particular would have been phoning friends, comparing notes or reassuring their son that they were fine but now they only had each other for company and they were reluctant to break the link.

Chloe tried to make the children rest but they refused to leave the crowded room for a bedroom and it was too cramped for them to lie on the floor.

Instead, they began making preparations for the next day. It was about a mile to the boatyard and they were going to take as many supplies as possible with them. Oliver swore that it was brighter by five o'clock the following morning. Maybe, the outline of buildings was a little clearer but it may have been just wishful thinking. However, Gladys insisted on listening to the broadcast.

It transmitted the same broadcast as before but added,

Will anyone able to produce qualifications in electronics or electrical engineering report to the nearest police station, or armed forces' depot. You and your immediate family will be given priority transport to the National Disaster Centre.

Warning. Anyone who falsely claims knowledge or experience in these fields may be liable to summary trial.

Will all police and armed service personnel also report to the nearest police station or armed forces' depot and place themselves under the command of the senior officer present.

All hospitals are closed except for triage posts. Only patients liable to respond to available services will be admitted. Patients with little hope of treatment in the present circumstances will be discharged.

There was a pause before the announcer spoke again,

We may not be able to broadcast for much longer. There's a mob outside accusing us of hoarding food. If it breaks in, then I don't know what will happen. God help us all.

"Are we ready to move?" Chloe asked, fear evident in her voice, "We must protect the children."

"We've got to protect ourselves as well." David pointed out, "If anything happens to Tom then we'll never get away."

Day 2

It was definitely lighter as they left. They made an odd sight. They were all bundled up in as much clothing as they could wear without being completely immobilised. Each pair carried garden poles on each shoulder and from the poles hung a selection of rubbish bags, plastic shopping bags and sheets all laden with the goods they thought they would need. They made their way in complete silence not daring to draw attention to themselves. It was almost too easy, reaching the boatyard with a sense of anti-climax. The security guard approached them as they stood by the gate.

"What's going on?" he asked, obviously scared, "All I've heard all night was that damned stupid emergency broadcast telling us to stay put. I should have been relieved at ten but no one turned up. I can't stay here for ever. The café's not open. Where can I get something to eat?"

"Let us in and we'll give you some food." Tom said, "Have you got any family?"

The security shook his head, "No, it's only me and my bed-sit."

"We're going to take one of those river-buses, stock it with supplies from that warehouse, head down river and try to ride this out. You can let us in and come with us or we can break in and go without you. Your choice."

David looked at Tom with new found respect. He had spoken confidently and with some authority without even raising his voice.

Tom felt more alive than since he retired. His ageing eyesight and stiff fingers had meant that he needed to ask for help on jobs that he should be able to do easily and it left him with idea that he was old and useless. Suddenly, he was back putting his lifetime of skills and knowledge to good use. It made him feel thirty years younger but considering that the circumstances were so grim, he almost felt guilty for being so happy.

Except for the lights dancing in the Northern sky, it had been the blackest night that the security guard had ever known. He guessed that they were the Aurora Borealis and guessed that they were connected to the solar flare. Although he spent ages watching them, fascinated by the sight, they did not distract him from the yells and screams from across the Thames and sometimes they seemed to come from just the other side of the Creek. Neither did they hide the myriad fires that he could see in all directions. He had felt safe inside the Creek's security fence though it was just an illusion. A determined gang could easily get in.

If David had seen Tom in a new light, then the guard had heard him with relief. Someone seemed to know what to do and had a plan. The guard wrestled with his conscience briefly, after all it was his duty to stop boats being taken and warehouses being broken into. However, he was not paid enough to go hungry and he would be one man against one of the gangs he feared were out on the rampage.

He unlocked the gate and they were in, being led to the guard's office.

"What happens now?" the guard asked.

"Tom chooses a boat and starts fitting it with extra water and fuel tanks." David said, "Emma and Jake keep watch. The rest of us can head for the warehouse. You sure it's got food in there?"

The guard nodded, "It's a cash-and-carry. It closed when the power went and the boss sent everyone home. He seemed more scared of his staff using the chance to pilfer stuff than anything else. He cycles in. It's nothing to do with fitness or ecology, just meanness."

"With luck it'll have sleeping bags and tents." David said, "We'll need them."

The guard nodded again.

"Traders get various discounts and VAT receipts but boats can tie up alongside it and stock up for a trip. I think the minimum purchase is two hundred and fifty pounds. That's not much if you're planning a cruise to the South of France."

"And we're going to steal much more than that." David laughed, "It seems right to me."

Tom and the guard looked uncomfortable at the mention of stealing but they both expected things to get far worse than the previous night and were keen to get out of London.

The tide was out but there was still a deep channel in the middle. It was bounded by soft, water saturated mud, impossible to walk on without getting stuck. A wooden walk way mounted on oil drums rested on the mud. When the tide came in, it would float. A small dinghy rested on a pontoon at the end of the walkway.

Two river-buses used for sightseeing were moored in the channel. They were waiting to be brought alongside the quay and lifted out of the water for the winter.

Tom slid the dinghy into the water and rowed out to the boat he had chosen. It was a modern twin hull vessel capable of carrying nearly five hundred people. The lower saloon could hold over two hundred and fifty. It already had a four thousand gallon water supply that would last them for a month or two if they were careful, and he was hopeful of fitting more tanks onto the top deck.

Breaking into the steering house was easy. He grinned, thinking back to other escapades when he was younger and more impulsive. Tom had a sneaking regard for David because the lad reminded him of himself as a youth.

The steering house looked more like a cockpit than a bridge but no matter. He settled into the pilot's seat and studied the controls. Satisfied, he pressed a button and he felt a reassuring tremor through the deck as the auxiliary engines came to life. Checking the readings he started the main engines.

Meanwhile, David and Steve, the security guard, had jimmied open the warehouse cautiously searching the dark tunnels between the stacks of goods. Gladys and Chloe were more business like. Accepting the inevitable they had armed themselves with shopping lists and were already piling flat bed trolleys with food. As one trolley was filled so Rory or Oliver pushed it out to the door and fetched another.

David filled another with batteries, sleeping bags and clothes. He found a section devoted to fishing. He had tried the sport but had never been very successful so he was not very interested in the rods, reels or line but the protective suits and thermal wear did catch his attention. He would mention the fishing tackle to Steve and Tom and leave it to them.

In another section, he found camping supplies, including radios that could be recharged by turning a handle on them. He was also surprised to find a supply of Arctic tents; double skinned to provide insulation and took a stock of them. David's thinking was that river-buses were intended for summer cruises and may not have very effective heating. In any case, heating took power and that was going to be limited.

They stopped for a break at eight o'clock, huddling in Steve's office listening to the radio. There was a lot less interference and the announcer could be heard clearly.

Following yesterday's solar flare, communications are still severely gridlocked. Remain in your own homes as much as possible. All aircraft are grounded. Train services are terminated and roads are blocked by abandoned cars.

Telephone systems have been severely damaged. There may be limited services in some areas but for the most part, they have ceased to function.

A person can survive two weeks or more without food but only a couple of days without water. Priority is being given to maintaining the water supply. Disregard previous instructions not to use toilets. Hygiene and cleanliness are essential to prevent disease.

If you are stranded, make your way to emergency camps that are being set up along major arterial routes out of cities. Disregard previous instructions to congregate on open ground. Please allow anyone stranded access to water and washing facilities.

You may enter unoccupied buildings to obtain washing and drinking facilities. You may also consume perishable goods while they are fit to eat. Taking any other property, including non perishable food will still be treated as looting.

That is the end of this announcement.

"We'd better hurry." said Tom, "Things are getting bad if they're condoning any sort of looting."

"Yes but it makes sense not to waste food, doesn't it?" Chloe asked.

"Sure but they've abandoned it." David said, "They don't expect to have the power back before it goes bad and what about those people in the parks. Last night they were going to be fed. Today they've got to get out of London."

"Have you seen a helicopter?" Oliver asked suddenly.

"No." Tom asked, "Why?"

"The roads are blocked, right?" Oliver explained, "What else could they use to sort London out?"

"Unless they're not trying to sort London out." Tom replied.

"Don't you think that we should have been arrested by now?" Gladys asked.

"You mean there should be a S.W.A.T. team coming down

ropes from helicopters ready to stop us from looting the place?" David asked.

Gladys nodded.

"I did hear a couple yesterday." Steve said, "I'd guess that they were over towards Buckingham Palace or Westminster."

"That figures." David sneered, "Get that lot out of London and forget the rest of us."

Chloe glared at him but stayed quiet, beginning to agree that they were being left to fend for themselves. She certainly felt easier about breaking into the warehouse. They went back to work. Tom brought the river-bus alongside the pontoon and helped Rory and Oliver to load supplies. Trying not to alarm the boys he kept a wary eye out for trouble after showing them how to release the cables securing it. The last thing he wanted was for it to be swamped by a gang intent on taking it over.

The early part of the morning had been quiet, almost peaceful but as the sun rose higher so they heard distant noises, screams, shouts, even gunshots again. Thankfully they all sounded distant but they seemed to come from all directions.

Jake and Emma were bored more than anything. The road had stayed deserted all morning and it was getting on for noon before they were disturbed.

Emma was taking her duties as lookout far more seriously and was the first to spot the group of men coming up the road. Jake, glad for something to do rushed off to find David while Emma hid behind some boxes watching the gate.

They reached the gate at about the same time as Steve. One of the men was Ray March.

"I'm the community defence coordinator." he said, "Open up. We need to collect any perishable food to distribute it."

"I'm not authorised to let anyone in." Steve replied, "I could lose my job."

"Haven't you heard the news?" Ray asked angrily, "We're authorised to consume perishable goods before they go off."

"Fair enough." Steve acknowledged, "But I'm not letting a gang like you loose on this property. I'll get my shift to stack it outside this fence and you come back later and collect it. I'm not opening this gate while there's a gang of you hanging around. The best thing you can do is to find a truck to carry it in. You'll never carry it all on your own."

Ray was sure that Steve worked alone but once again he was rattled by someone who seemed to be handling the situation. Everyone else, including Ray himself was scared, uncertain about what was happening, not knowing for sure what to do.

"OK." he said, "We'll do it your way but I'm warning you, we'll smash through the fence if we have to."

Steve shrugged, "Don't worry. I agree that it's daft letting all this food go to waste. Let's just do it properly."

Steve turned and looked around. The path was hidden by a yacht laid up on a cradle. A shed and a pile of junk hid the entrance to the cash-and-carry warehouse that they were using. Anyone outside the fence might get a glimpse of one of the boys pushing trolleys but that was all.

It was the least of their problems because just then they heard shouts from across the Creek and saw a gang of youths picking their way through the junk yard located there.

"Time to be moving," Tom said.

"Not yet." David replied, "There's no boat on that side. They'll have to go up Archibald Avenue then round past Marchy's gang. Does that thing have a horn?"

Tom nodded.

"I'll tell Emma to head straight for the boat if she sees anyone else and when you see her make as much noise as you can. That's the cue to drop everything and come running."

"Jake and Oliver can stand by those ropes, ready to undo them and we get clear of this jetty fast."

Tom ignored the lack of nautical terms and nodded. They paused at one o'clock to listen to the news, gathering in Steve's office.

This is the Emergency Broadcasting Service Announcement. It is being broadcast on all operational public and commercial radio channels.

Work has already begun to maintain the water supply. Clean water should be available for the foreseeable future. Cleanliness and hygiene remain top priorities. Use as much water as you need to stay clean.

Communities cut off from government control may make whatever arrangements they wish to ration food supplies. If you enter unoccupied premises, please do the minimum damage to secure essential supplies.

Do not loot electrical goods, motor vehicles or other unessential items.

Stay calm. Remember, if you have clean water you can survive for up to three weeks without food. We have a hundred days stock and we are planning a nationwide distribution programme.

If you have shelter and water stay where you are. We will get you food as soon as we can.

That is the end of this announcement.

Even Chloe seemed shocked.

"We still haven't seen a helicopter, have we?" Gladys asked, "Surely they should be all over the place dropping food parcels. Where are they?"

"My guess is that they're conserving fuel." Tom said, "They could be worried about air traffic control as well. I reckon they're holding back while they plan this food distribution."

They all fell silent for a moment. Chloe frowned.

Twenty-four hours ago she had been concerned with making a good impression with her bosses. Emma and Oliver were there to demonstrate how she stood for good middle class family standards. More than any of the others she had been dependent on electricity and suddenly it was no more. She couldn't phone work to say that she could not get in. She could not call it up over the Internet either. Her washing machine, dish washer and central heating were useless. In short, everything that showed her to be a smart, up-and-coming business woman were gone.

She was not a bad mother, just a little less interested than she might have been. Now Oliver was being listened to as some sort of expert. It confused her, as well as making her proud at the same time and she was following a lout and self confessed thief into her own life of crime. The problem was that every time she had tried to maintain standards or try to get some control of the situation, a radio announcement or some other event undermined her. Each time she was left with the feeling that David was right and knew what he was doing. She was in a state of shock desperately trying to remain calm.

To their surprise they were able to work until mid afternoon. The top deck boasted rows of water tanks, Steve had scavenged other boats and found fuel containers, which also littered the deck. No one seemed to know where they were going to be filled. Tom just smiled and tapped the side of nose as if to say, I know what I'm doing.

High tide had passed and the water was dropping but there was still plenty in the Creek.

Suddenly Emma came haring down the walkway and as arranged, Tom sounded the horn. Chloe and Gladys grabbed the trolleys that they were filling and hurried towards the walkway. David headed for the gate, careful to stay out of sight.

A group of men were heading their way. They seemed to be armed and more importantly, David recognised some of Ray March's men as well the youths that he had spotted earlier, across the Creek. It seemed as if they had stopped, startled by the boat's horn but they recovered their wits and were hurrying forward again.

The gang ignored the boat yard, hurried across the cash-and-carry's car park to attack the main entrance. David ran back to the walkway. Gladys and Chloe were loading the last of the supplies from the trolley onto the boat.

"Is everyone here?" David asked.

Chloe nodded.

"Steve's helping the boys with the ropes." she said, "We're nearly done."

"Get on board now." David snapped, "I don't want them charging onto the pontoon while we're still struggling to untie."

As they clambered aboard, two men burst out of the rear entrance that they had been using, saw them and yelled for help.

Jake and Rory struggled with the bow mooring but the stern was already clear of the pontoon as the first of the men reached the walkway. Tom put the boat into reverse taking the strain off of the bow cable and the boys slipped it clear. By the time the men were on the pontoon, there was clear water between the boat and the pontoon.

Tom allowed the boat to ease out to the middle of the creek before going ahead. It swung effortlessly to point to the entrance to the Creek and picked up speed leaving the gang to yell angrily but uselessly at them.

Instead of heading downstream as they had discussed, Tom headed upstream making for a raft with two incongruous looking fuel pumps and a small office looking like a security guard's hut. Three deserted work boats were tied up

With Steve guiding the boys, they managed to tie up alongside the raft.

"We'll probably have to hand crank them." Tom said, "I'll show you what to do then I'll look for the water valve. Let's hope the broadcasts are right about water supplies keeping going."

For the rest of the afternoon they transferred fuel, filling the main tanks first before filling the assortment of containers stacked on the top deck. It was getting dark before they were finished.

They felt safe on the river. Amongst the supplies that Steve had loaded was a barbecue and charcoal, which he fired up on a space that they had set aside on the upper deck. The strange surroundings, their sense of achievement in spite of their tiredness and their sense of security all help to make it a party atmosphere. Even the children's excited chatter helped drown out the occasional shouts and screams from the shore.

Afterwards they switched on the radio to hear the latest announcement. Their usual station was silent but after switching around the channels found another one. There was a lot of background noise but they could understand the announcer.

This is the Emergency Broadcasting Service Announcement. It is being broadcast on all operational public and commercial radio channels.

Communications are still being severely disrupted. The government is attempting to maintain the mains water supply. Please do not attack engineers and helicopters engaged in this work. They do not carry food with them and the aircrews are authorised to shoot anyone attempting to board their aircraft.

If the engineers fail to maintain the water supply then you face dying of thirst or from the diseases that will come from contaminated sources.

Food supplies are being organised. It is slow because it is being set up without the aid of modern communications. Ration your food supply: it may have to last for a month or more. If you have seed then use any available ground for planting.

Remember there is nothing to be gained by leaving your homes. If you do, then you could be exposing yourselves to greater danger. If you leave, you may find yourself without food, without water, without accommodation and without protection.

There were no known casualties caused by exposure to the solar flare. There were some casualties due to equipment failure.

Most aircraft landed safely. Ships are continuing to dock. Roads are being cleared. Even if you cannot see it, work is being done to help you. Attacking radio stations will hinder that work. Attacking repair teams will not help. Rioting of any description will not help.

Stay tuned to this wavelength, stay calm and stay in your own homes.

Here are the main points again.

Food supplies are severely disrupted but they are not destroyed. Please be patient and ration food locally available so that it can last for a month or more.

Although the situation is very grave, please stay calm and please be patient.

We shall repeat this broadcast in an hour's time. Stay tuned to this wavelength, but switch your radios off now to save your batteries until we come on the air again. That is the end of this broadcast.

"I'm glad we followed your advice, David." Gladys said, "It does sound as if things are getting bad. How did you know?"

David laughed.

"I thought I was just lucky to start with. You know, somewhere to hide from the filth...." he glanced at Chloe, "Police then a chance to slip away for a while. Those announcements bothered me but it was the March geezer that decided it. If he thought he had a chance to run everything, then I knew that things were bad."

"There's another place I think we should visit." Tom said, "I reckon now's a good time and it's just for Steve, David and myself."

Everyone looked at him.

Night 2

"I reckon that we need guns and ammo." he continued, "Shotguns would be best. You don't have to be a good shot to do some damage."

"Where are we going find them?" Steve asked.

Tom grinned.

"You can still find just about anything on the river if you know where to look. There's a group of gun shops. They've got a pretty smart one in the Regent Street area and a couple of others that sells second-hand and reconditioned ones, plus of course mail order and ammunition. Now the thing is, they're pretty cagey about where their warehouse and workshops are."

"And you just happen to know?" Steve asked.

Tom nodded, "Ask any of the locals and they'd say it was a furniture warehouse and so it is - at the front. We're going in through the back."

"It's going to be well protected, isn't it?" David asked.

"In normal times, if a boat gets a bit close, alarms go off and the police would arrive in minutes. The quay is set back a bit and there's a chain mounted on buoys to deter casual visitors. It all looks low key but these aren't normal times. Without the high tech electronics its protection probably is as low key as it looks and I reckon we should take a look and see what's what."

"OK!" David said, "You can show me how to use the outboard motor."

"I'll show you and Steve how to row." Tom exclaimed, "It's silent and this isn't the sort of trip where we want to attract attention That's why we're not using one of those other boats."

"Aye, Aye, Cap'n." David laughed giving Tom a mock salute, "As long as you're not going to stand over us with a whip."

"It's a thought." Tom replied, grinning just as happily, "If it wasn't for this fucking arthritis I'd show the pair of you."

He turned to wife, "I'm sorry dear, It does get me down at times."

It was uncanny how Tom could find his way. The moon was bright and the Northern sky still shimmered with coloured lights though they were dimmer than the previous night. Despite his arthritis he was alert, constantly looking around for danger. It was strange how deserted the river was and he wondered why more people weren't leaving by boat. It occurred to him that most people were still following government advice. Not many people would be near their own boats and they would still need to stock them with food. Their own little group had been extremely lucky in knowing what to do before anyone else had thought about it.

Even so there could be other traffic on the river and he had no wish to be run down by it. He smiled with satisfaction; he had found the building he was looking for and it had not changed. David and Steve were pulling well together and it was easy for him to grab one of the buoys while Steve picked up a pair bolt cutters to sever the chain.

They tied up alongside a rusty old ladder. So far there had been no alarms or challenging shouts. They clambered the ladder to reach a door in the wall. It was old and David was able to quickly jemmy it open. He looked at the bag of tools and welding equipment that Tom had brought. David wondered about the old man's past. He certainly seemed to know what he was doing when it came to breaking and entering.

It was hard work hauling the gas bottles up especially when Tom spoke sharply if anyone made too much noise. Finally, everything was in a short passage way, blocked by a steel plate.

"When we stopped handling cargoes a lot of the men got out." Tom explained, "One or two got into security work but we all got together in the pub and chatted about work, the way we used to. That's how I learnt about this place. It's a listed building so they can't change the outside which is probably why it hasn't been turned into flats. There's other stuff but it'll keep.

"The security isn't designed to keep people out, it's designed to slow them down until the police get here. If you're a terrorist armed with plastic explosives it would be easy but why would terrorists want to waste that sort of explosives for a few sporting guns and black powder. In normal times we'd have been picked up by half a dozen cameras when we reached the buoy. By the time we got through that plate the River Police would have got our boat. There'd be armed police on the other side, but now all we've got to do is to burn off those bolt heads and pull it clear."

There were three domed heads on each side of the plate. Because they were round, they could not use a spanner, which was why Tom had brought gas welding equipment. Telling the other two to turn away in case of sparks he donned a pair of goggles and got busy. It seemed to David that the procedure was taking hours. But Tom was satisfied. He even took the time to cut a slot in the plate for a handhold.

"David, you're the young strong one." he chuckled, "See if you can pull it out."

It shifted easily, too easily in fact, nearly falling on top of them. It took the three of them to manoeuvre it round to lean against the wall. After that, it was easy. The passageway led to a store-room that held guns and ammunition. They selected shotguns and Tom selected the correct sized cartridges before the others hauled it all up the passage to the outer door.

"My folk used to go hop picking when I was a kid." Tom explained, "A local farmer taught me how to shoot and I've done a bit of clay pigeon shooting over the years."

"Of course." Steve said drily, "Is there anything you haven't done?"

"Let's get a move on." David snapped, "We need to get back."

The others nodded and got back to work. To David's way of thinking, the dinghy was dangerously overloaded on the return journey but Tom did not seem worried. *He's not doing any of the rowing,* David thought to himself, *He doesn't have to worry.*

As they neared the river-bus, Tom tensed. He could see a strange boat tied up beside it. The tide had just turned and was ebbing so Tom let the dinghy drift silently down to the raft. Working as quietly as he could, he loaded the guns.

They weren't spotted and they paused, uncertain what to do. David climbed onto the raft and crept across to the river-bus. Still he was not spotted, though he saw a shadowy figure standing at one of the entrances.

"Come back in." he heard Chloe's voice command, "I don't want you falling overboard or something."

David relaxed, grinning at Oliver's exasperated oath muttered under his breath. He made a lousy lookout anyway so it did not matter whether he carried on standing guard or not. David wanted to be sure though so he quietly clambered on board and peered inside.

Two young men in their twenties were lying, securely tied on the floor. A girl of a similar age, was also similarly tied. Rory was standing over them holding a length of pipe.

A second girl, heavily pregnant was sitting on a bench between Gladys and Chloe with Gladys apparently checking her temperature, pulse and listening for the baby's heartbeat.

"Hi, we're back." David announced as he entered the saloon.

Oliver rushed across to hug him.

"They tried to stick us up," he gabbled, "but we stopped them."

"Explanations later." David snapped, "Ollie, Jake and Rory come help us."

"It's OK." he called out as he clambered out onto the raft, "Bring the dinghy round."

Tom made sure that the guns were safe and then complied, hauling it around instead of rowing before quickly unloading.

"OK, what's the story?" Tom asked when they were all settled down.

"Rory was supposed to be lookout," Chloe said, "but he didn't see their boat until it was too late. They came rushing in, swearing and waving those knives around. Anyway they worked us back away from the supplies. A couple of them tried helping themselves while the other two kept us covered but they had forgotten Rory. He threw that pipe at them and yelled."

"That's right." Rory interrupted, "Gladys and the others charged and overpowered them."

David knelt down beside one of the strangers.

"Now you, what's your story?" he asked gently.

"Fuck you." the stranger snarled, "You can't tie us like this. We've got rights."

"You had rights." David said gently, "We can pick you up and drop you over the side. Who would notice?"

"That's murder. You can't do that." the man yelled struggling helplessly.

"Who would notice?" David asked again quietly, "What's your story?"

The man stopped struggling, he looked defeated.

"We'd come up to town to do some shopping. Jessica needed some more baby gear. I offered to drive her and Damien up. Lily came along for the ride. When we got back to the car, the power cut had started and we couldn't even get out of the car park. We've got friends in Kingston so we tried walking there. We got as far as the Chelsea Embankment before it started getting dark. The pavements were packed. There was this gang. They had torches and they picked out one girl."

He shuddered, "She screamed but they wouldn't let her go. We turned back and another group seemed to follow us. We sneaked down onto a pier and found a rowing boat. We would have pushed off but we managed to hide because they got interested in the bigger boats and started breaking into them. They found some booze and they were out of it by dawn. I managed to grab some bottled water and some blankets from one of the boats they had looted but we were pretty cold by then. We didn't dare try to take Jessica past them back up to the road so we tried rowing.

"Like I said we were pretty cold by then and we just tied up to a buoy wrapped the blankets round us and tried to get warm. By the time we were spotted by anyone, the tide was on its way out. We didn't have the strength to row against it so we just tried to stay in the middle of the river, out of reach. By the time we figured we should do something it was getting dark again and then we spotted you. We watched you for a time and saw you three guys row away. We took a chance to grab some food."

"And you just happened to be carrying knives?" David asked quietly.

"I didn't know what to do. When I grabbed the water I grabbed some knives as well. I should have grabbed some food but I didn't think of it. I wanted a drink, to get warm and I was scared for Jessica. It was stupid but I think I was too scared to be hungry."

"It makes sense." Tom said, "It could have been the early stages of hypothermia causing him to be a bit confused."

"What are you going to do with us?" Damien asked looking scared.

"We should hand you over to the police for breaking in like that." Chloe snapped. She hesitated as she noticed that everyone, including her own children were laughing at her.

"Did you see any police?" Gladys asked before turning to the prisoners, "What's your name, by the way?"

"I'm Craig." he answered, "I tried asking a couple of cops for help but they couldn't do anything. They'd left their car in the jam. Their radios were out and they were trying to reach the nearest station. They were being mobbed by people like us who needed help. As it got worse, they couldn't have arrested anyone. They'd have been taking on whole gangs without back up."

"How did we do for supplies?" David asked, "Remember we've got five extra mouths to feed."

"Five?" Steve queried.

"Those four and the baby."

"We can't take in just anyone." Chloe exclaimed, "The food won't last and we've got children to protect."

Everyone turned to David.

"If we don't take them then the kindest thing to do is to drop them over the side like I said." he said, "A quick drowning's better than slow starvation. How are we off for supplies?"

"I kept tabs on what we brought on board. A bit of Navy training." Tom grinned, "I reckon we're down from a year's supplies to eight months."

"We haven't slept much in the last couple of days." David said, "Let's try to get some now. At dawn, we'll head back to the Creek. Tom, Steve and myself will take one of those work boats and some shotguns to cover Damien and Craig while they reconnoitre the warehouse. We've done our share of gathering food. If you lot want some, you get more."

"And who put you in charge?" Craig asked.

"David has known what to do since it started." Gladys said, "You'll do well to listen to him."

"We don't have much choice while we're all tied up, do we?" Craig retorted.

"We'll have to take it in turns standing guard." David said, "Let's try to make sure that we don't have any more unwanted visitors and don't let this lot cause trouble."

"Ollie, Jake and Rory," David rasped out, "you take it in turns keeping the adult's company. Let's get some sleep."

"Please call Oliver by his proper name." Chloe said, "The children need a routine. They should go to bed at the proper time."

Chloe looked put out. David did not care whether it was because he was disturbing her son's rest or not calling him Oliver.

"I never thought that I'd say this but I'd love a bit of my own routine. A night in a cell, breakfast and a nice chat with a couple of cops. If it happens again, then you can get the kids back into their routine. Until then, they help when they're needed and tonight they help by helping the sentries to stay awake. Ollie can come with me and I'm not going to spend all night calling him Oliver."

Chloe glared at David beginning to hate him. It was bad enough that she was taking an unplanned holiday from work and was travelling in a stolen boat. She was trying to protect her children from an uncouth lout and was losing the battle. No one supported her and she could not figure out how to do things better than him.

She contented herself with kissing Emma and Oliver good night and telling them to go straight to bed if they got tired. Oliver tolerated the briefest contact before hurrying over to sit with David.

"Why aren't you scared?" Oliver asked.

"I am scared." David said, "I wish a helicopter would show up, tell us that we've got it all wrong and arrest us for stealing this lot. I just don't think it's going to happen. Your mum does though."

You don't like her, do you?"

"She's trying to look after you. That's cool but she thinks I'm dirt and you're all better than me."

"I think you're cool." Oliver said. He lay down on the seat, rested his head on David's thigh and promptly fell asleep. David was uncertain what to do. In his old world, Oliver acted gay enough around him to get beaten up but given Chloe's protective manner he wondered whether Oliver even knew what sex was. He smiled to himself. That had to be an exaggeration but he was sure that Oliver's attitude was innocent.

Gladys had watched the little scene played out.

"He's got a bad case of hero worship, hasn't he?" she smiled, "He could do worse."

"His mother thinks I'm rubbish. She might be right."

"Tom spent time in a borstal when he was about your age." Gladys said, "He's not turned out to badly, has he?"

David smiled, "No, but shouldn't Ollie be acting all tough? He seems a bit soft."

"You mean queer." Gladys said, "I know how these things work and nothing's changed since Tom's day. Oliver reassurance from someone he trusts and he's chosen you. Let him cuddle up to you, sit on your lap or whatever. He'll be more relaxed and when you need him, he'll be there for you. Nothing sinister, just hero worship as I said."

For David, he felt accepted by people in a way that he had never been before. They trusted him, not seeing his gentleness as weakness. He eased, himself from under Oliver to unroll a sleeping bag making do with a blanket over him rather than climbing in. Oliver awoke just enough to see what was happening, and slid over to lay beside him and still Gladys just smiled indulgently. David's emotions suddenly crystallised into a completely new sensation. He wrapped an arm protectively round the boy and fell asleep knowing that there was someone who depended on him.

Craig, Damien and Lily spent an uncomfortable night lying bound on the floor. Jessica joined them laying down on one of the bench seats. Jessica might have released them but she felt safe with Chloe and Gladys fussing over her and Damien was only too willing to keep her happy.

Craig was not fond of some street kid being in charge but he had to admit that they had stumbled onto a pretty good set up for getting through the unfolding disaster. They had heard the hourly broadcasts that Gladys insisted on listening to. They had heard Chloe and Gladys talking about how conserving food had gone from fourteen days to a month and was now for as long as possible.

Now that he was warm and fed, Craig realised even more just how lucky they had been so far. Getting themselves trapped on the pier, being reluctant to push off for so long had put them at risk and he could not see his captors making the same mistakes.

Feeling safe made a terrific difference so he did not argue too strongly. Only Lily opposed staying. She was determined to get home and despised David for his background. She did not rate Tom and Gladys much higher and only just tolerated Chloe.

David and Oliver took the last watch. They had both slept better than they thought possible and were cheerful and alert in the cold night just before dawn. David sent Oliver to wake everyone just as it began to get light. Gladys was on familiar territory as she began breakfast. Jake and Emma, glad to feel useful, helped. In between their own food, they managed to feed the prisoners.

Day 3

"I think they've got something to say to you." Gladys told David.

"Take this boat up to Teddington Lock." Lily said, "Hand it over to the authorities and we won't say anything about how we've been treated."

"Shut up, Lily." Craig snapped, "It would still be thirty miles overland to get home. We'd never make it."

"Of course we would." Lily snapped back, "Once whoever is in charge at Teddington knows who Daddy is then he'll get us home."

"I doubt whether High Court judges carry much weigh, at the moment." Craig said.

"Daddy always said that if you gave them half a chance then the great unwashed would bring this country down. I must say, I'm surprised that you're siding with them Craig."

"Maybe Lily has a point." Chloe said trying to sound sensible, "If we headed up river, we'll probably find someone in charge. We'll be safe then."

"Exactly!" beamed Lily.

"No we won't." Oliver piped up, "Things are still getting worse. You've heard the announcements. They're not letting TV back on to save fuel. They don't know when they'll sort the food arrangements and they keep warning that if they keep on attacking the water people then London will lose its supply."

"Be quiet, Oliver." Chloe snapped, "Stop interrupting the grown ups. You don't know what you're talking about."

"Yes, I do." Oliver shouted, "You keep saying that but you're the one that doesn't. If you'd had your way, we'd be in doors waiting for Ray March to feed us. And I'm going with Tom and David."

"You're not." Chloe yelled, "You'll go and sit on that bench until you learn some manners."

Oliver stood still, "No. I'm going to help David."

"Have you ever fired a shotgun?" David asked.

Oliver shook his head.

"Neither have I." David grinned, "I reckon that Tom will only want only one learner in a small boat. Can anyone else shoot?"

"We can of course." Lily replied, "It's a part of country life but I don't expect you to understand that."

"I suppose you'd object if I dropped her overboard like I suggested, wouldn't you Craig?" David asked.

Craig caught the mixture of anger and amusement in David's eyes.

"I would but I'd understand." he said, "Lily, shut up. We didn't do too well on our own. I trust David but I'd feel happier if you untied us."

"Ollie, untie Craig and Damien." David ordered, "I'm sorry, Lily but I'm worried that you might try something stupid while I'm gone."

David paused, "Now we've finished breakfast, we should get going. Rory and Oliver, keep lookout in the wheelhouse while we're gone. If you see anyone approaching, sound the horn."

"And while you're gone, I'll show them how to fire the guns." Gladys said.

Everyone looked at her startled, except Tom.

"I told you." he explained, "I did some clay pigeon shooting. I didn't like to mention that Gladys used to come along because she was a better shot than me."

It was not much but the chuckles that that followed his remark lightened the atmosphere. They were all a little more cheerful as they began their preparations.

They changed their plans slightly. Damien had done some sailing so they took two boats, each trailing a dinghy. Once in the Creek, they moored one of the boats to a buoy before tying the second one alongside the pontoon. Picking up his shotgun Tom relaxed on the deck covering the pontoon and walkway.

David and Steve piled into the dinghy and rowed to a point where they could cover the entrance to the warehouse. David expected to see someone on lookout duty but the place was deserted. Damien and Craig headed for the entrance, on the alert for an ambush.

They entered the building carefully. Soon they were back hauling the trolleys laden with boxes. Damien seemed to have concentrated on baby supplies but Craig was hauling food. Before long, the first boat was full. It had been taken out to be moored in the Creek and the second one was now tied up to the pontoon.

They worked, uninterrupted, for nearly three hours before the scavengers came rushing out of the warehouse, running for the boat. Moments later men chased out after them. Steve fired his gun into the air before lowering it to point at the men. David followed his lead and aimed as well. The men got the message and dived for cover.

Damien and Craig quickly slipped the line and cleared the pontoon, bearing down on the other work boat allowing Damien just enough time to transfer. Again Tom slowed long enough for David to catch the line that he threw, then with the dinghy secured, Steve and David climbed on board.

They looked around. A gang of about ten men were standing, watching them.

"You know, I feel bad about taking that food." Craig said as he watched them, "We're leaving them to starve."

"If that food is distributed fairly then it'll keep them alive for an extra couple of hours." David said, "They're from the estate and they've got all those blocks of flats to feed. It's impossible. It'll keep us alive for months. You might not like it but it's much more useful here. If we stay alive, we may be able to help them."

"What about Ray March?" Tom asked.

"None of his mates were there." David said, "I expect that he's finished by now."

They didn't speak again, lost in their own thoughts and were still in a sombre mood when they reached the river-bus. David was the first to realise that something was wrong and nudged Tom.

The third work boat was missing and Gladys was standing on the upper deck with her arms wrapped around Oliver who was hugging her tightly. Rory and Jake were standing by the deck-house with Jessica. Tom waved and Gladys waved back.

"I reckon it's safe." Tom said, "We'll tie up and the other boat can cover us."

As Tom jumped up onto the raft, Gladys hurried over to greet them with Oliver close behind her. He stood close to David who instinctively put his arms around his shoulders.

"Chloe released Lily and they took the other boat." Gladys said breathlessly, "They took some fuel but didn't take any food or water. Lily said that they were going up to Teddington to get help. They seemed certain that if they could get far enough out of London then they'd meet up with some soldiers or something. Chloe took

Emma and tried dragging Oliver on board but he refused. He was screaming that they were safer with us, she was screaming that we were going to get ourselves arrested and I was worried that we would attract attention."

"We've been lucky so far." David agreed, "I'm surprised there's no one else on the river."

"I expect that there's still easy pickings on shore." Tom said, "We were pretty quick off the mark, thanks to David. Watermen would be in the wrong place just the same as everyone else."

"Can we go after Mum, please?" Oliver begged, still visibly upset.

"Do you remember when I threatened to break Rory's legs if he tried to leave?" David asked.

Oliver nodded.

"Well, if he had gone, we couldn't have helped him if he'd got into trouble." David continued, "I came on heavy because kids are always trying to prove how tough they are on the estate and you just slap them down but at least they do as they're told. I can't make your Mum do as she's told, especially now that she's listening to Lily. Even if we went after them do you think we could make them do as they're told?"

Oliver shook his head, sobbing unashamedly.

"I didn't think that I'd be able to help my Mother either." David said sadly, "We've got to be strong enough to pick up the pieces when we get the chance."

"That's what I tried to tell her," Oliver said, "but she wouldn't listen."

"You and Craig can take one of the other boats, some supplies and a couple of guns." David continued, "I won't stop you if you want to go after them. We're still heading down river and hiding out in the marshes around the Estuary."

Oliver looked at Craig who realised that David had put him on the spot. Still unhappy taking orders from David, but at the same still terrified by events, he was just glad that he was with people who knew what to do. Lily's plan might work if they could reach someone in authority but who knew what was happening at Teddington? If it was as out of control as Chelsea then three females alone would be in real trouble. Would himself and a boy be able to do much more?

"They might come to their senses." he said, "How long can we wait here in case they come back?"

"I don't think we can." Gladys said, "There's been people watching us on the opposite bank. Are they likely to find a boat?"

"Oh yes." Tom replied, "I'm amazed that there weren't any guards at the warehouse."

"There were a couple," Damien said, "but they'd set up house in the booze department. We got them taped up while they were still out of it. We were OK until someone came to check up on them."

"Had they taken much stuff?" David asked.

Craig shook his head, "They trashed the place and it looks as if they were more interested in the drink. Apart from that, I reckon they took more electrical goods than anything. If I said they weren't taking it all seriously, would that make sense?"

"You mean they're still expecting everything to get back to normal and just taking advantage while they can?" David asked.

Craig nodded, "Yeah. And we saw some stains on the path outside. I reckon it could be blood."

"Ray March made a lot of enemies." David said, "If he's finished then all that food is going to go to waste. We can't stop it but I don't feel so bad about taking some of it."

"If we're careful, we've got enough to last through the Winter." Tom said, "I still say we should head down river to Sheerness. There are a load of mudflats and small islands in the Medway. We could hide there and be safe. We could take on a few extra people who're willing to fit into that plan but if they choose not to then we're not strong enough to go on hare-brained rescue trips."

"We're talking in circles." Jessica said, "Oliver, Craig, I'm sorry. I've got my own kid to think about and there're these three. I think we should head down stream."

"It's the logical thing to do." Oliver said, still close to tears, "Could we start the engines and be ready to get away if there's trouble but hang on in case they come back, please?"

David nodded, "It's a plan. I don't think eating in public is a good idea. We'll eat in shifts with a couple on top keeping lookout."

Tom and Damien secured the work boats for towing after loading the dinghys onto them. The riverbanks were eerily quiet but Tom had heard at least a dozen shots in the distance. There was still the occasional shout or scream but otherwise it was a peaceful early Autumn afternoon.

For once, even David was reluctant to act. Like everyone else, he had hoped that everything would quickly get back to normal. He had expected to be returning to his mother's flat and reassuring her while she found out which of her dealers was still around. Once they set off, it would seem like he was finally abandoning her. They gathered on the stairs to listen to the latest bulletin. Mostly they were still out of sight but the guards could hear it as well.

This is the Emergency Broadcasting Service Announcement. It is being broadcast on all operational public and commercial radio channels.

Communications are still severely disrupted. The government is attempting to maintain the mains water supply. Please do not attack the engineers and helicopters engaged in this work. They do not carry food with them and the aircrews are authorised to shoot anyone attempting to board the aircraft. If the engineers fail to maintain the water supply then you face dying of thirst or from the diseases that will come from contaminated sources. Remember, you can survive for weeks without food but only a day or two without water. The government's priority is to supply water.

Food supplies are being organised. It is slow because it is being set up without the aid of modern communications. In the meantime, ration your food supply: it may have to last for a month or more. Work with your neighbours to ration any locally available food.

If you have seed then use any available ground for planting.

Remember there is nothing to be gained by leaving your homes. If you do, then you could be exposing yourselves to greater danger. If you leave, you may find yourself without food, without water, without accommodation and without protection.

There were no known casualties caused by exposure to the solar flare. There were some casualties due to equipment failure. Most aircraft landed safely. Ships are continuing to dock. Roads are being cleared. Even if you cannot see it, work is being done to help you. Attacking radio stations will hinder that work. Attacking repair teams will hinder that work. Rioting of any description will hinder that work.

Roadblocks are being set up around towns and cities. Only those who can prove that they have somewhere to go will be allowed to leave. Looting has been extended to include the theft of farm livestock and crops. Looters may be shot on sight.

Stay calm and stay in your own homes.

Here are the main points again.

Food distribution is severely disrupted but supplies are not destroyed. Please be patient and ration food locally available so that it can last for as long as possible.

Although the situation is very grave, please stay calm and please be patient.

The following information is being broadcast on London transmitters only

Camps are being set up around the M25. No one will be allowed to travel further without a permit. You will be held in a camp while it is being processed.

This station is running on standby generators and we are running short of fuel. We may have to shut down until fresh stocks arrive. If the soldiers guarding us are not withdrawn and fuel does arrive then we will remain on air.

We shall repeat this broadcast in an hour's time. Stay tuned to this wavelength, but switch your radios off now to save your batteries until we come on the air again.

That is the end of this broadcast.

"Mum's going to come against those roadblocks, isn't she?" Oliver asked, "What's going to happen to her? She's got nowhere to go out of London."

"We'll hang on here until dusk, if we can." Tom said, "Then we head down river. If anyone wants trouble, then the Thames Barrier will be the place. We'll be low down and with luck, anyone on the barrier caissons will be silhouetted against the sky. Once through, we'll aim at getting to the M25 Dartford crossing about half an hour before dawn. We'll throttle back to just above steerage way and let the tide take us through. My guess is that they'll be concentrating on the town and not the river. It's half a mile wide at that point so with the engines at just over tick over they probably won't hear us."

"Yes but what about, Mum and Emma." Oliver persisted.

"Teddington is well inside the M25." David said quietly, "I'm sorry Ollie but your Mum's put them in real danger."

Craig nodded grimly.

"He's right." he said, "That bit about the M25 was a real

shocker. It sounded as if they were abandoning everything inside it. We've got to get out while we still can."

Oliver burst into tears clutching David and hanging on tightly. David looked surprised and tentatively put his arms around the boy.

Uncertain what to say or do, he tried, "When things get better we'll go and look for them. We know where they're going so it won't be too difficult."

Tom looked on approvingly, confusing David again. He was still thinking of his old world, Oliver's emotions would be a weakness to be exploited and David would lose face by appearing soft. Here, he was still gaining creditability.

The river was still quiet. They were still fairly close to the centre of London so Tom guessed that boats upstream would be trying to get further up the river rather than head into the city and similarly for those downstream.

In either case, most boats would be about to be laid up for the winter so few would be stocked with food or fuel. They were probably still one of the best organised crews anywhere on the river. Things would change when supplies began to run low or when lack of water or disease added to the panic but for now they were keeping out of trouble.

The first real disturbance occurred mid afternoon when a helicopter flew over them. It was the first bit of air traffic that they had seen since the disaster had started. They watched as the helicopter turned then slowed, dropping down to hover alongside the raft allowing a police officer, armed and in full riot gear to jump out.

The helicopter rose back up and circled, allowing more armed police to cover the raft.

David, whispered something to Gladys who nodded then he picked up a shot gun, loaded it then left it broken as he crooked it over his arm as Tom had showed him. Other adults followed suit as he clambered out to greet the policeman.

"Is this your boat, sir?" A very feminine voice shouted over the noise of the helicopter.

Instinctively, David needed to be cheeky, to put one over on the authorities. He cupped his hand around his ear pretending that he had not heard. She tried again and this time David just shrugged. Admitting defeat she signalled to the helicopter to back off more.

"Is this your boat, sir?" she asked for the third time.

45

"No." David said in his normal tone of voice, "Why do you want to know?"

The police woman knew that David was trying to wind her up but why? They were not desperate like other groups that she had contacted and in spite of the guns, they were not aggressive so what was going on?

"Why don't you come inside and have a cuppa?" David shouted so that she could hear, "We'll make one for your friends as well."

The scene was bizarre becoming surreal as the boys appeared with a camping table and set a tray upon it complete with crockery, a dish of biscuits and a jug of milk. Gladys appeared a few moments later with a massive teapot also putting it on the table.

The police woman was still trying to decide how to react when the others disappeared into the boat's saloon leaving David waiting for her by the door.

She shrugged. Seeing the shotguns had frightened her. Her crew had already been fired upon and were wary. These people had made it clear that they knew how to handle guns but were still not hostile. She shrugged again in defeat, turned towards the helicopter gesturing to them to help themselves and followed the others into the saloon.

"Is this your boat?" she asked yet again.

"No." David replied, "A couple of days ago you could have arrested us for boat-napping or whatever it's called."

"I still can." she retorted, "It's not emergency supplies."

"Yes, it is." David exclaimed, "We're neighbours and we're rationing our supplies to last for as long as possible. If we can do that surely we can take something to carry it in?"

"Do you intend staying here?"

David paused as the helicopter got noisier. A second policeman jumped off. The police woman went to the door and waved. The other policeman relaxed and headed for the table. He picked up the tray and carried it to the helicopter which moved away again.

"We're heading down to the River Medway." David replied when he could be heard again.

"You won't be allowed outside the M25 boundary." she said.

"Are they blockading the river?" David asked, "Besides we

can prove that we've got somewhere to go."

The helicopter moved in again and a police officer got out heading nervously for the saloon. The police woman got up to greet him and they whispered quietly.

The policeman returned to the helicopter and it flew off up river.

"It's coming back for me later." she explained, "There's trouble at a pumping station near Barnes. They want me here because of your guns."

"What are you going to do, arrest us?" Craig asked.

The police woman laughed, "I think that's the idea. They just don't know how to handle things at the moment. It's a gut reaction to worry about people with guns in the city but they haven't got the resources to do anything. If there's a problem, then I'm supposed to radio in."

"Are your radios working?" Oliver asked.

"Yes but we have to keep them switched off except for an emergency. We're running on standby generators back at base and we have to conserve fuel. Satellites are gone so none of the tracking works. Fibre optic telecommunications are working where equipment hasn't been damaged. A lot of stuff had battery backup but without electricity it's not being recharged."

"Like your radios." Oliver said brightly.

The police woman nodded, "The electricity companies have got spares for a few substations blowing and they constantly order more in. Thousands of them have blown. Computerised stock control and ordering has gone. The factories are closed anyway so there's just not enough to repair the system. That doesn't include the ones that are lost because the tracking is down."

"Surely someone's working on it." Gladys said.

"Yes they are," the police woman replied, "but the big fear is typhus or cholera or something. That's why they're concentrating on the water supply. Even that's computerised so it relies on communications. That's without fuel being stolen, and equipment being smashed out of pure frustration.

"One of my colleagues managed to email her sister in Canada and get a reply. I can't phone my mother in the next street. It's all so patchy and without finding spares, then getting them to the right place, it's going to get worse."

"My mum's taken my sister in a boat up river." Oliver said, "Will they be all right?"

"It wasn't a good idea." she replied, "There're gangs looting boats and reports of shooting at anything moving on the river."

"Do you know anything about down river?" David asked.

"There're troops guarding Tilbury docks and the Navy's got patrol boats on the river. It's to protect shipping so they shouldn't bother you. There're rumours that they're going to turn it into a supply centre so don't go too close."

"So things are getting moving again." Gladys said, "Maybe things will be OK after all. What's your name, dear."

"Julie." she replied, "Things are going to get worse. With the Internet down they can't get records of what's in the containers. They've got to open each one and inspect it. There's no power for cranes to shift them, River pilots, tug crews and dock workers are scattered. There're other problems but I don't want to go through the whole briefing. The only safe way of shifting supplies is by helicopter. Lorries have already been hijacked."

Julie continued, "It's why I'm not going to stop you. You're not going to add to the problems and there's one way I can help you. We can't get I.D. cards printed at the moment so we use a password. At the moment, it's Doomsday."

"That seems appropriate." Tom laughed.

Where Oliver seemed to latch onto David, proud that an adult finally took him seriously, Jake and Rory still felt lost and among strangers. They kept close together content to act as lookouts on the top deck away from the others. They took their job very seriously and the others felt safe enough when they were on watch.

Suddenly Jake came crashing into the saloon, announcing that a couple of boats were approaching from the opposite bank. Everyone, including Julie grabbed their guns and rushed out onto the raft. David pointed his gun into the air and fired high above the approaching boats.

Julie was confused. As a police officer she should not be condoning this but her experiences over the last couple of days had deeply upset her. The boats were inflatables with outboard motors and they veered off at the gunshot. She was sure that she had seen a glint of metal suggesting the crews were also armed.

David realised that they had made a tactical error as one of the boats circled round behind the river-bus out of sight. A second shotgun blasted out. He glanced around, noticing for the first time that Oliver, Rory and Jake were missing.

"We should get under cover." Julie said, "They may have guns."

As a second gunshot rang out she added, "You'd better see what's happening."

The second dinghy reappeared. It's bow seemed oddly misshapen and two of its crew were bailing furiously. A man on the first boat stood up and while struggling to keep his balance aimed a gun at them and fired. No one even heard the bullet but Julie dropped to the deck of the raft, legs splayed out and gun aimed at the gunman in typical marksman fashion. The others simply aimed at him.

The inflatable was still nudging closer with one revolver against a police machine gun and four shotguns. It was the man handling the outboard motor who lost his nerve first. He opened the throttle and turned the boat away, desperately trying to get out of range. As the boat turned, the gunman nearly lost his balance completely and as he struggled not to fall overboard, dropped the gun into the water.

It was enough and the two boats retreated to the bank.

Leaving Jake and Rory on sentry duty, the rest returned to the saloon and compared notes.

It was Oliver who had noticed how unprotected they had left themselves and had told Rory to pick up a gun and follow him. As the second boat approached, he fired his own gun into the water just ahead of the inflatable.

Rory and Jake watched fascinated as the patch of water briefly turned into a seething cauldron but it had not deterred the boat. Oliver aimed carefully and fired again, blasting the fabric bows of the inflatable. Some stray shot struck one of the crew making him yelp, but he was not seriously injured. It was enough for the crew though and they retreated.

"I don't think we should stay here, any longer." Tom said, "Next time they come, we may have to kill someone."

Julie disappeared on deck fiddling with her radio when she returned, she seemed upset.

"I've radioed for back up." she explained, "The helicopter's been damaged. It can't pick me up until tomorrow. I'm to

49

commandeer this boat and shelter here overnight."

"We're not staying." David said firmly, "What happened?"

"Someone took a pot shot and cut a fuel line. It was on the ground at the time and they taped it up. Apparently there was a bit of a gun battle and the sniper was killed. Now they've got to check for other damage and repair the fuel line properly."

"They can f..." David glanced at Gladys, "They can go do something nasty to themselves. We could leave you a sleeping bag and some food so that you could spend the night on the raft or you could come with us. We'll put you on one of those patrol boats, you mentioned."

David's complete contempt for authority was disconcerting. She should be threatening to arrest him for obstruction but it was impractical. It was worse because his alternatives were far more sensible than her orders.

"I'll come down river with you." she said, "I'll radio through and then I'm ready."

They agreed that they should not remain tied up any longer even though Oliver had pleaded for them to wait in case his mother returned. Tom compromised by agreeing to take them up river in case Chloe and Lily were trying to get back. He made it clear that he would only go as far as Tower Bridge, the first bridge on the river.

He also insisted that anyone who could handle a gun should be on the top deck, ready for trouble. Huge banners hung from the railings acting as screens. Julie made them squat down so that they were hidden behind the rail. It did not offer any protection but they could not be seen except from a high angle.

Tom was uneasy. He could see people on the banks, watching the river-bus go by. They were quiet but any one of them could turn into a threat. It was eerie how the city that he had lived in all his life had suddenly become such hostile territory. They were still the only vessel using the river so at least there were not more gangs ready to race out to board them pirate fashion.

The river was getting too narrow for comfort as they rounded the final bend. Tom scanned the bridge with his binoculars. With the river traffic so light he did not expect it to be guarded. He was worried about people desperate enough to try to jump aboard and those angry at the way their lives had been destroyed could drop anything from slabs of concrete to grenades onto the deck. Beyond was H.M.S. Belfast. The warship itself was not a threat but it effectively halved the width of the river.

Tom slowed the boat until it just had steerage way. He opened the wheelhouse door and called for David, Craig and Oliver and described his worries. He looked at Oliver

"We've always been in range of a sniper or something." he added, "And we're getting closer to the banks all the time. As we get close to the bridge, they'll be able to throw stuff at us. Oliver, Craig, it's your folk we've come for. Can we risk going further?"

Oliver was close to tears as he shook his head.

"That's only the first bridge, isn't it?" he whispered.

Tom nodded.

"Yes." He answered, "We might get up to Teddington without trouble but…"

"But we've got these kids, Jessica and the women to think about." Craig interrupted, "Do what you think is best."

"What's that?" David suddenly called out, pointing towards the bridge as a boat emerged from under it. Tom snatched up the binoculars.

"It's them." he confirmed opening up the throttle.

Just then a second boat appeared, apparently chasing them. Luckily for Lily and the others the other boat was not much faster than theirs. Tom opened the throttles and steered towards the approaching craft. A shotgun blasted off but no one could see who had fired.

The river-bus was not designed for speed but it looked impressive as it bore down on the approaching boats. The lead boat continued resolutely towards them but the chase boat veered off slightly then continued on course. Tom slowed again letting the bus drift towards the work boat. Lily misjudged it completely, forgetting that boats did not have brakes and scraped down the side of the river-bus. Remembering the small boats that he was towing Tom swung round in as sharp a turn that he dared.

Under Julie's directions the rest were all checking their guns.

The chase boat was an open dinghy powered by an outboard motor. Tom positioned the river-bus between Lily's boat and their pursuer. Water pushed out by the turn, the river-bus's wash and turbulence caused the dinghy to rock violently.

Peering over the rail, Julie looked at the two men. She was

certain that one of them had a hand gun. Yelling instructions at her team the men suddenly found themselves facing a broadside of shotguns at close range. It was enough. The boat veered away, continued turning and headed back up river

It was not going to be easy to catch the work boat. As Oliver glanced down into it, he could only see Lily and his sister, Emma.

"Slow down." Tom yelled, "Just enough so you can steer."

Oliver relayed the instructions. Tom slowed the river-bus as well as he eased it past the other boat. Realising that she was safe Lily recovered her composure then finally obeying Oliver's shouts, she eased back on the throttle. Now that he could close the gap without the wash either swamping the smaller boat or just pushing them apart he waited until they were close enough and ordered Oliver to throw them a line.

Once the line was secured, the situation was under control. Lily cut the boat's engine and helped Oliver to get Emma onto the bus before scrambling aboard herself. Tom opened the throttles of the river-bus and they headed down river.

Leaving Jake and Rory on watch, the rest hurried into the cabin to hear Lily's story.

They had taken their boat through the centre of London without incident getting as far as Chelsea but then they began to see other boats heading up river. Others were beginning to see the river as a route to safety and had got the same idea. As they rounded a bend, they saw a number of boats stopped just before a bridge. People were milling about on the bridge and as they got closer they saw a rope tied to oil drums, stretching to a bridge support on the other side of the river. It left a single bridge span for the boats to pass through.

One of the boats edged too close to the improvised boom and shots rang out. A couple of other boats replied but when one of the sailors fell into the water, it all went silent again. Two boats got the message and tied up beside a pontoon while the crews meekly allowed their stores to be carried ashore before being allowed to proceed under the bridge.

A fast powerboat went next. It got close to the pontoon then gunned its engines. They heard a single shot fired. The boat had begun to turn to line up with the opening but just continued to turn and drove into the bank. Lily saw a man with a rifle stand up from where he had been hiding behind some boxes on the pontoon and watched as an inflatable nudged alongside the stricken boat and a couple of men jumped aboard. They heard more shots, then watched three bodies being thrown overboard.

"We can hide the guns." Lily said, "They can see that we're not carrying food. Just look pretty. Men always fall for it and they'll let us through."

Before Chloe could reply Lily had opened the throttle and was steering towards the pontoon. At least, Lily had enough sense to stop a little clear of the pontoon. The work boat was open except for a wheel house and even that was open at the back. Lily smiled sweetly at the men on the pontoon.

"I'm just trying to get home to Daddy." she said, "We're not carrying anything."

Chloe could see the lust in the men's eyes and at least one of them was studying Emma closely.

"Get us out of here." she whispered.

"You stay put." one of men snapped drawing a gun, "You've got taxes to pay. If you can't pay in food, then you can pay in some other way. Throw my mate a line and he'll pull you in."

Chloe bent down as if to comply but grabbed a shotgun. She brought it up aiming wildly and fired. She was not holding the gun properly and the recoil slammed it into her shoulder making her stagger backwards. An instant later, the man with the gun fired striking Chloe in the chest.

One man was grabbing his face where some shot had pulped it, screaming as he slid to the ground. Blood was pouring from the throat of a man standing just behind him. He was probably already dead as he fell backwards.

Blood was pouring into Chloe's damaged lung but she was still conscious. She staggered backwards again struggling to keep her balance. She might have succeeded but Lily opened the throttle and spun the wheel. Chloe lost her struggle as the boat moved under her and she fell overboard.

The man fired again but the shot went wild. Emma was screaming for her mother who was struggling in the water. The man turned his frustration to her and fired again. Chloe's struggles stopped and she just floated, face down.

The man with the gun and another ran for the dinghy to give

chase.

The dinghy was just a little faster than the work boat, slowly catching up. Lily kept glancing over shoulder and if they got too close would blast at them with the shotgun while Emma held the wheel. The gunman in the dinghy was not an expert shot. Lily was used to shotguns. They stayed far enough apart for the gunman to need the luckiest of hits to do any damage while Lily was invariably on target. The buckshot was too widely spread to do much harm but it was enough to maintain the stand-off.

"When are you going to grow up, you stupid bitch?" Craig yelled as Lily and Emma finished their story.

"It wasn't my fault." Lily sobbed, "I've still got money. If Chloe hadn't panicked, we would have got through."

"They weren't after money, dear." Gladys said quietly, "Three females in these conditions. How do you really think they wanted paying?"

Everyone looked at her.

"Surely you don't count Emma?" Damien asked.

"Oh yes." Julie replied, "I'm willing to bet that there's quite a market for her already."

"You still shouldn't have called me a bitch." Lily said still sobbing, "How can I get in touch with Daddy now? I just want to go home."

"So did Chloe." Craig said, still angry, "And you let her die before she could say goodbye to Oliver."

"Once Chloe was in the water, Lily was right to leave," David said calmly, "She would have got Emma and herself killed if she had stayed. I can't believe she didn't know what those pervs wanted though."

"I've known her since school." Jessica said, She probably thought that a bit of flirting would have got them through."

"Well, why not?" Lily replied, "Once I'd got their attention, I'd have given them the money and explained that Daddy would help them get out of London."

"No, dear." Gladys said, "Not as things are now. Money is worthless and your father can't do anything. They would have raped you and Chloe, possibly even Emma then dumped your bodies in the water."

Lily turned deathly white. Of all the group, she was having the hardest time accepting events. She could not openly admit it but she now understood just how stupid she had been but she still needed the notion that her father would sort everything out

"I need some air." Craig snapped, "David, Why don't we relieve Jake and Rory?"

"I don't know what I saw in her." Craig continued once they were on deck, "She's such an airhead."

David grinned.

"I know what you saw. They're trying to pop out of her jumper. Don't all you rich kids want to run home to Daddy?"

"No more than you street kids are all on drugs." Craig riposted before continuing, "My parents are at their villa in Provence. Dad'll be tending his grape vines and Mum will think oil lamps are wonderfully rustic. Don't laugh but I do wish that I was with them. I think that if anyone can get through this then they can."

"In that case I wish I was with them as well, mate." David laughed, "Even if I was only the hired help."

"Instead, I'm the help and you're the boss." Craig said, "It's a funny old world."

Night 3

Jake approached them.

"Tom is getting worried about the next hazard." he announced

David and Craig glanced at the wheelhouse. Tom was sitting impassively, guiding the river-bus down the river. Even as they turned to look at him he leant out, looked back and beckoned them forwards.

"We're coming up to the Thames Barrier." he said, "I haven't seen any boats heading down river so I don't suppose that they'll block it in any way. The thing is, it'll only need one man on one of the piers to give us real trouble."

"What do you suggest?" David asked.

"It's getting dark and the tide's about midway." Tom replied, "Let's stick to what I suggested earlier. We stay as quiet as possible, throttle back to just above steerage, all lights off. I'll aim for the centre gate and slip through. If there's trouble then I'll open it up and go through at full speed."

"Sounds OK." David said, "But I think that I should lead the way in one of the work boats. If they have blocked it, then it'll be better than risking this thing."

"Good idea." Craig said, "But it's a job for the help, not the boss. Damien can help me."

"Not Damien." David said, "Oliver and Rory can go with you."

"They're kids." Craig exclaimed, "You can't put them in danger like that."

"Jessica and Gladys are looking after Emma." David said, "Oliver needs something to do and Rory is older. They will all have to take their fair share of the risks. Even Jake will stay on deck with a shotgun like the others."

"Is this a street gang thing?" Craig asked, "You know, initiating new members or something."

"No." David snapped angrily, "It's a manpower thing or don't you want to be covered by as many guns as possible?"

"Sorry." Craig answered contritely, "I don't know what made me say that. I suppose I was brought up to think kids shouldn't get involved in grown up stuff."

"In Napoleonic times boys as young as eight served on warships going into action." Tom said, making everyone stare at him, "Officers started their training as Midshipmen at twelve. I agree with Craig that it wasn't right and I agree with David that we need as much gun power as possible. We don't have to kill anyone, just scare them."

"We still shouldn't even go that far." Craig said.

"It's too late to discuss it, lads." Tom said, "We're coming up to the bend. We need all the lights out now and whoever goes in the launch needs to get ready. Move it."

"Who's the boss?" David grinned as they hurried off.

As they made their preparations, Rory stood shyly in front of David.

"Are these any good." he asked holding up a couple of two way radios.

David nodded, not daring to ask where Rory had found them. With everything else on their minds no one had thought to organise a proper search of the bus; they had just searched for what they needed. Jake and Rory had got bored and started exploring. They had found the radios in a cabin right at the back of the boat that had served as some sort of staff room.

"We'll do a couple of tests then you can switch yours off." David said, "We don't need it coming to life while you're sailing through the barrier."

He turned to Jake to ask if there were any more. Jake nodded and David sent him to take one to Tom.

With everything ready they rounded the last bend and crept towards the barrier. The launch pulled ahead. It was a clear cloudless night. With no man made lights, there were more stars visible than even Tom had ever seen. A half moon shone to their right. Buildings were silhouetted against the sky and Tom could even pick out moored barges but the water was black.

Everyone without a particular job, even Jessica and Emma, was crouched behind the railings holding a shotgun. It was cold and uncomfortable and the tension made it feel even more uncomfortable. Suddenly David's radio crackled into life.

"We're through the barrier." Craig said, "They haven't blocked it and I didn't see anyone."

David felt relieved but knew that they still had to be cautious. According to Tom there were service tunnels connecting the piers. As long as there was fuel to power the on-site generators, they could be pumped out making the piers safe refuges; small islands in the river, serviced by the tunnels or small boats. There was a clatter as Lily put her gun down and headed for the saloon. Suddenly the saloon lights came on.

Swearing out loud David rushed for the saloon almost diving for the light switch.

"What the fucking hell do you think you're doing, you stupid bitch." he yelled almost ready to punch her.

"I heard Craig tell you that it was all clear." Lily said, "I'm not waiting for a foul mouthed oik like you to give me permission to get in the warm."

"Oik?" David asked, briefly amused but then Craig's angry voice sounded over the radio.

"What the hell are you playing at." he snarled, "You've woken everyone up, you stupid idiots."

"Satisfied?" David asked as he rushed for the stairs to the top deck.

"Craig, get out of range and when I say, turn all your lights on and fire a few shots into the air." David snapped out, "If your diversion distracts them at the right time we may still get through without anyone getting hurt."

By now David had reached the wheelhouse.

"Tom, let's hope that they haven't got snipers." he said, "The lights are off again so let's keep silent until we're about fifty metres from the barrier. Craig can make his diversion and then we'll go through at full speed."

"We won't open fire unless they do and we'll try to fire over their heads."

He gathered his gunmen around him.

"I don't know much about guns." he said, "But we want to scare them, not kill them. Hold your fire until I give the order then fire a single shot. I'll wait a second and give the order again. Reload as quickly as you can and wait for my order. If I shout 'down', then aim at them. It'll all depend on how good they are with guns."

He paused sensing the tension, "Oh and afterwards, Julie can arrest us all for disturbing the peace."

He heard the chuckles as Julie retorted, "I'm not sure how I arrest myself."

"This is no laughing matter." Lily snapped who had followed David back up to the deck, "Damien, you've done officer training. You take charge."

"OK!" Damien said, "We've got a plan, pre-arranged signals and a clear chain of command. Let's do it."

"We're in position." Tom called out from the wheelhouse and David radioed Craig.

They dimly heard a whoosh before the river in front of them was lit up in an eerie red glow. Oliver had found a box of flares and they had fired one. Tom opened the throttle wide and the river-bus surged forwards. They heard the blasts of Craig's crew's shotguns. After the silence and blackness of the last couple of nights, the sudden pandemonium worked.

All eyes on the barrier piers were staring downstream as the river-bus powered through. Suddenly there were shouts from the piers and they could dimly see people rushing towards them.

"Fire." David roared out, and a hail of shot screamed over the pier defender's head making them all duck. A second single shot rang out and a man screamed. Lily grunted in satisfaction

"Keep it above their heads. FIRE." David yelled.

They were through. Someone on the piers may have fired at them but nothing had come close. Once they were safely clear Tom slowed and switched on all the navigation lights.

While the others secured the launch and welcomed Craig and the boys back, Julie went over to Lily.

"I'm arresting you for attempted murder, causing death through negligence and discharging a weapon without authority." she said reaching for her handcuffs, "You do not have to say anything, but it may harm your defence if you do not mention when questioned something that you may later rely on in court. Anything you do say may be given in evidence."

The others looked on, stunned.

"I don't know what sort of legal system we'll have after this," Julie explained, "but someone got injured back there and it was unnecessary. Those people are trying to make the best of things, just like we are. It was her blatant disregard of your advice that got Chloe killed and by disobeying your orders she put us all at risk. David's plans require the minimum force necessary to defend ourselves and that has always been legal. Lily is just a menace to herself, you and others."

"I don't suppose this boat's got a cell." Craig said, "I'll help you guard her."

"So will I." Damien agreed, "What do you say, David?"

"I've come fu…" as always he glanced at Gladys, "I've come close to shooting her. You're not serious about my plans being legal, are you?"

"A few days ago there'd be Armed Response Units ready to shoot you down if you even sneezed after all this." Julie replied, "Now, I don't know. What I do know is, that bloody woman is a menace and I've restrained her in the only way I understand. I'll release her if you like."

David laughed.

"A few days ago, your mates were chasing me in a stolen car." he said, "Now I'm the duty officer. We'll hold her until we meet up with the Navy boat and we'll get rid of her. You're welcome to stay if you want to."

"Thanks." Julie answered, "How about listening to the news. If it gets much worse, then I may take you up on that."

The broadcast began with the now familiar announcement though it was a different station and was far weaker with a different voice.

This is the Emergency Broadcasting Service Announcement. It is being broadcast on all operational public and commercial radio channels.

Communications are still being severely disrupted. The government can no longer maintain the mains water supply in the following cities, London, Birmingham, Manchester, Liverpool, Sheffield and Glasgow. We urge residents in those cities to stop the gangs who are impeding our work. Helicopters are engaged in transporting essential personnel. They do not carry food when overflying towns or cities so it is pointless to attack them.

If you do not restore order then you should conserve as much water as possible, make arrangements to dispose of bodily wastes and to burn bodies.

If you have seed then use any available ground for planting.

Remember there is nothing to be gained by leaving your

homes. If you leave, you may find yourself without food, without water, without accommodation and without protection. You will not be allowed through the cordons set up around towns and cities. If you attempt to break through, then you will be shot.

Food supplies are being organised. It is slow because it is being set up without the aid of modern communications. In the meantime, ration your food supply: it may have to last for some considerable time. Work with your neighbours to ration any locally available food.

Ships are continuing to dock. Roads are being cleared. Even if you cannot see it, work is being done to help you. Attacking radio stations will hinder that work. Attacking repair teams will hinder that work. Rioting of any description will hinder that work.

Looting has been extended to include the theft of farm livestock and crops. Looters may be shot on sight.

Stay calm and stay in your own homes.

Here are the main points again.

Although the situation is very grave, please stay calm and please be patient. The following information is being broadcast on London transmitters only.

Camps are being set up around the M25. No one will be allowed to travel further without a permit. You will be held in a camp while it is being processed. If you try to cross the M25, you will be shot.

We shall repeat this broadcast in an hour's time. Stay tuned to this wavelength, but switch your radios off now to save your batteries until we come on the air again.

That is the end of this broadcast.

"I think I might be staying with you." Julie said quietly, "It's getting worse out there."

"The next problem is the Navy blockade at Dartford." David said, "Will they let us out?"

"I don't know." Julie replied, "We're organised and equipped. I reckon that we've got a chance."

"Tom's going to adjust our speed so that we get there about dawn." David said, "We'll pair up and do a watch each while the rest of us get some sleep. Ollie do you want to team up with me again?"

Oliver nodded enthusiastically.

"What are you going to do about Tom?" Julie asked, "He's the only one who hasn't had any rest. Gladys is getting worried about him."

"Once we're past Dartford, we'll park, anchor or whatever we do in this thing and Tom can sleep for as long as he needs." David said, "When he's ready he can start teaching Craig and Damien how to drive. I want you to think about defending this thing better. By the way, does anyone know what to do when Jessica's baby comes?"

He slept fitfully for the next couple of hours until Gladys woke him, "Tom says it's getting light and he can see the bridge. I've got your breakfast ready."

Every one else seemed to be awake and waiting for him.

"Rory, you, Jake and Oliver, go on deck and take a good look around. Take Emma with you if she's up to it." he ordered, "Take a good look around and see if you can spot anything wrong."

"That's nice of you." Jessica said, "Making them feel useful."

"Emma will remember what it was like up river." David said, "She might be able read the situation better. Jake and Rory know how to keep their eyes open and look for things. Tom, Julie and Damien aren't stupid but different points of view might help."

There was a touch of frost when David went on deck. There was a definite glow in the Eastern sky and the bridge was silhouetted against it. He could see the river banks clearly enough but at that moment the bends in the river were taking them parallel to the bridge instead of towards it.

Jake came running over.

"Tom says we'll be there in about twenty minutes. We haven't seen anything but we're coming up to the last turn."

Julie approached him next.

"Do you want everyone on deck and armed?" she asked.

"Good idea." David replied then, thinking of a war film he had once seen, added, "Carry on please."

David headed for the wheelhouse.

Day 4

"Morning Tom," he said.

"Good morning, David." Tom replied, "Is everything ready?"

David nodded, "Do you think that we should switch the radios on? Maybe we're taking this power saving a bit too far."

"I don't know." Tom replied, "This thing's fitted with AIS."

Seeing David's puzzled look, he added, "Automatic Identification System. I don't suppose there's many left to track us but it seemed safer not to risk it."

"At the moment we might be hidden from their radar by the houses on the bank." David said, "Once we're round the bend they'll probably see us. Keep the radio off though. Thinking about it there maybe other boats trying to get through. They may be able to listen in. I don't want them knowing how we're stocked up. If the Navy wants to talk to us, then it can do it face to face."

"It makes sense." Tom agreed.

"As soon as you can manage without lights, we'll turn everything off." David grinned, "Maybe they've only got a rowing boat after all."

At first, it seemed as if they were in luck but as they neared the Dartford Crossing it was light enough for them to see the sleek frigate moored up river from it and a fast inflatable approaching them. A number of other craft were also moored up though few seemed to be manned.

"We'll need our secret weapon for this." David said, "Oliver, go and tell Gladys to make breakfast for our guests."

He looked around.

"Julie, I want three guns up here to cover their boat. Everyone else head for the saloon. Hide the guns and hang around by the entrance. We can't stop them coming aboard but they've got a script to follow and if we let them do that then we'll never get through. I just want to slow things enough to get them off the script."

David waited by the entry gate until the inflatable was secured alongside. There were four armed men covering the river-bus and an officer. David held out his hand to help the officer aboard.

"Good morning." David said, "Welcome aboard. Come inside

and get warm. Bring your men if you like. Would you like some breakfast?"

"I'm Sub Lieutenant Carlisle." he replied, "Thanks for your offer but I'm afraid that I must place you all under arrest. Who's in charge here?"

"I am. I'm David." he replied, "You're still welcome to come in and sit down while we discuss this. There's one or two problems you'll have to sort out first."

David was right about unsettling his visitor. By now, it was a well practised operation. He would board, put them under arrest, listen politely to their angry demands for their rights then quietly take them ashore to the camp with a promise of some hot food and a safe place to sleep. Few were used to challenging authority and most were relieved to feel that someone was back in charge.

David was used to being arrested and it took skilled questioning by an experienced officer to undermine his air of confidence and bravado. They were standing on a tiny deck. Behind David was the entrance to the saloon and to his side were steps to the upper deck while on his other side, a bulkhead. With Craig and Damien behind David, the Sub Lieutenant felt very cramped, suddenly uncertain of himself.

"We will open fire if you resist," he said, trying to regain control.

"We're not resisting." David replied, "And if you do open fire, you'll be shooting at a pregnant woman, children and a police officer. Is it worth starting a gun battle when we could settle this over some warm food?"

Sub Lieutenant Carlisle gave in. He ordered his men to stand clear and cover the wheelhouse then followed David and the others into the saloon. He stared at the stacks of supplies before settling down at the table David indicated. Gladys appeared with a plate of bacon and eggs for their guest and coffee for them both.

It had been a long night and Sub Lieutenant Carlisle was hungry. He ate hungrily and sat back relaxed while David waited patiently.

"OK." David began, "First, we've got supplies to last for six months and we're going to hide out in the islands in the river Medway. Second we have a prisoner on board who was legally arrested by a police officer. If you now arrest the police woman what happens to that arrest? Third, the police officer is trying to report for duty. Technically she's commandeered this boat and we're acting under her orders. How can you arrest us for that?"

"I'd need to talk to this police officer first then speak to the Captain." Sub Lieutenant Carlisle replied.

David had noticed Oliver watching them intently. He beckoned him over and told him to take the Sub Lieutenant to Julie. David sat contentedly back knowing that he had guessed right. The Naval officer knew less about the law than he did and he was as scared as everyone else.

Sub Lieutenant returned, saluted and said, "The Captain sends his compliments sir, and invites you aboard to speak to him."

"OK." David replied, "Do you have a doctor on board?"

"Yes sir." Sub Lieutenant Carlisle replied.

"While I'm over there, could he come over here and check on Jessica, please?"

Tom steered towards the warship while Lieutenant Carlisle returned to the inflatable and resumed his patrol.

"You don't need a hostage," Commander Richards grinned as they greeted each other.

"It never crossed my mind." David replied, "This is the last chance that Jessica will have to be seen by a doctor."

"I see." the Commander said, "We're invited to the Wardroom to discuss your assessment of the situation."

"Why me?" David asked.

"According to Sub Lieutenant Carlisle, your people think that you're some sort of whiz kid." Commander Richards replied as they sat down, "My orders aren't secret. They're to defend the dock facilities on this neck of the river and to stop anyone from breaking the cordon. We've not been trained for anything like this so any input is useful."

Not only the Captain but all the officers gathered there and even Petty Officers and Ordinary Seamen had been invited. They were all watching him intently.

"I keep getting treated like some sort of genius or leader but I'm not." David responded, "My science expert is a thirteen year old kid who tells me that electrical spikes blew most of the equipment in the electricity supply. There were spares for the occasional breakdown but not enough to repair more than a tiny part of the supply now. Without power how do they make more?"

"And you think it will take six months to get back to normal?" one of the officers asked, "That's what you're planning for, isn't it?"

"I don't think it'll ever get back to normal." David replied, "I noticed a load of containers over there. What's in them? Food? The spares they need? You're defending it. Do you know anyone who knows now that the computers are down?"

Everyone stayed silent.

"I think that your assessment is correct." the Commander said, "Some of the crew live in London. How bad is it there."

"It's pretty bad." David replied, "I haven't seen or heard anything good since the power failed. The gangs are dangerous. We were lucky to be on the river so we were pretty much isolated from it all."

"I understand." Commander Richards said, "The reason members of other messes have been invited is because they still have families in London. Is there any chance of getting them out?"

David shook his head.

"So far as I can tell, it's run by gangs now. They've got guns and we headed down stream because the river gets wider. It's harder to block and there're no bridges. Except here of course. Everyone was scattered. The schools didn't know whether to send kids home or hang onto them, adults out at work just had to try walk home. There's four kids on my boat. I've told them to keep their mobiles charged and check for messages. There's nothing out there at the moment and I doubt if there ever will be again. It's just the only thing I could think of."

"It's easy for you to say." one of the sailors said, "You're getting your family out."

"Mum's a smackhead." David said, almost tearfully, "I bumped into people who could think straight and I'm here. If I'd gone back to her, I'd be starving like the rest of them."

"So you didn't even try." the seaman persisted.

"Try what?" David persisted, "Find her enough drugs so she could walk out of London?"

"Yes but she's family." the seaman said angrily, "You should have done something."

"That's enough." Commander Richards snapped but David interrupted.

"No, that's all right." he sobbed, "The police were looking for me because of a stolen car so I had to lie low anyway. If it had been a short power cut, she probably wouldn't have noticed and I'd still be dodging the police. By the time I knew how big this was, it was too late. I suppose I could have broken into a shop, stolen some food and tried to carry it past the gangs up to her flat but what odds would you have given on me?"

As the rest absorbed the implications of what David had said, the silence made him feel uncomfortable.

"What are your plans now?" Commander Richards asked.

"We've only got one waterman and he needs sleep. Once he's ready, we'll head on down river." David replied.

"Would you be prepared to remain here for a few days?" Commander Richards asked, "I can issue you and your crew rations and refuel your boat. I'd like your evaluation of the situation here."

"There is no situation." David said, "There hasn't been since they started talking about cordons around towns. How many troops have you got to do your bit?"

"So if you were in my position, what would you do?" Commander Richards asked.

"Fill this ship with as much food and fuel as you can carry. Stuff it up the gun barrels if you have to. Then put to sea and stay there until you can make a difference."

"I meant deal with the situation here." Commander Richards answered quietly, "How much of a threat is the River. How many would try to escape in this direction."

"Forget your Navy charts. Take a look at a road map." David retorted, "Your docks here are surrounded. Tom showed me that when we heard you were here. How many men do you have? Assuming that you could arrange a food convoy. How would it be protected once it was out of the dock?"

"OK." Commander Richards conceded, "I do have some discretion but I'm supposed to keep the food stock available for the official distribution."

"OK, here's the hard question." David said, "You have food supplies. Should you feed one person for a hundred days or a hundred people for one day?"

"The point being that more supplies might not come for ninety-nine days." Commander Richards said, "It's playing God with a lot of people's lives."

"Or playing government." David exclaimed, "By the way, where is the government?"

"That is classified." Commander Richards answered seriously, "Let's just say in a hastily opened bunker intended for World War Three somewhere in England."

"In other words, holed up behind a lot of troops and barbed wire with no idea what to do."

Commander Richards stayed silent. He was getting uncomfortable with David's appraisal of the situation. He felt as if he was being drawn to the conclusion that he should abandon his duty and orders, to save his crew.

"Excuse me, sir." an officer said, "Maybe we should come up with a contingency plan in case there's a complete breakdown. If things aren't as bad as Mr. Robson suggests, then we shelve it. If they're as bad or worse, then we're ready. How long do you think we have, sir."

Still unused to being addressed so formally, David would not have answered if the officer had not turned to look at him. He shrugged.

"As long as you can hold those containers." he replied, "I don't care if I break the law. Can you, if you have to, Captain. What's it called, mutiny?"

"You don't pull any punches, do you?" Commander Richards asked, "Very well. We'll hold these facilities for as long as we can or for as long as the Government appears functional. We'll commandeer a suitable cargo ship and start transferring essential supplies to it and we'll start searching the containers. That stays within my current orders. Lieutenant Scales, work with Mr. Robson and come up with your contingency plans. I think you'll have to accept that the worse the situation gets, the fewer people you can save."

Before Commander Richards escorted David back to the gangway, they went to the Captain's cabin.

"I do have some top secret messages." Commander Richards said, "I shouldn't tell you this but the breakdown is happening faster than anyone imagined it could. You're right, there are not enough troops and the cordons are a joke. People just want to get out of the cities. In many cases they're commuters who want to get home and who can blame them.

"One crew member lives in Hornchurch. It's only six miles away. He just can't accept that we can't help his family. If he shoots his mouth off one more time, I'll have to confine him."

"Six miles?" David exclaimed, "Don't these things have helicopters that you could send?"

"One's been assigned to other duties. The other was undergoing a major service. It's serviceable now but it's on standby for other duties as well."

David grinned.

"I've never stolen a helicopter." he said, "Now that would do my cred some good. Of course, you would never go against orders would you?"

Commander Richards stared at David thoughtfully for a moment then picked up a telephone.

"Lieutenant Scales. We need to know what's really happening out there. Organise a helicopter patrol over Hornchurch would you please? O.S. Smith knows the area. Attach him to the flight crew. If it's appropriate you may pick up civilians for a further debriefing."

He turned back to David.

"Very well. You've convinced me to stretch my orders to the limit. It may do morale some good to at least try to save some of our families."

Back on the river-bus, everyone crowded around him wanting to know what had happened. David repeated the discussions he had. They agreed that it would make sense to stay for a while. They heard the roar of a helicopter taking off and shortly after Lieutenant Scales asked to come aboard.

"The Captain is more worried than he'll admit." the Lieutenant said, "You rattled him with your talk of the Government breaking down. I don't suppose that any of us liked it but it always comes down to it being his decision. I think he's testing the waters with this unauthorised helicopter flight. If Air Traffic Control doesn't notice, he may do more. It's one way of testing the Government's control."

David nodded, "I imagined officers to be stiffs who would never go against orders."

"You do get them," Lieutenant Scales acknowledged, "but Commander Richards is OK. Now any thoughts on a contingency plan?"

"How about Sheerness docks?" Tom suggested, "There was a

Royal Naval Dockyard and it has the remains of defences going back to Napoleonic Times. Sheerness itself is on the Isle of Sheppey and that's only connected to the mainland by a couple of bridges. Establish a bridgehead in the docks then extend the perimeter according to the defences we can use and the food we can distribute."

David got bored listening to Tom and Lieutenant Scales planning the occupation of the docks. He wandered onto the top deck to be alone and clear his head. He was still sitting on the deck when the helicopter returned. He watched the crew hurrying into the bowels of the frigate. He was just beginning to feel a little chilly when a seaman approached him, stood smartly to attention, asking him if he could visit Commander Richards.

The frigate's captain looked shaken when David arrived. He gestured David to a seat and sat quietly for a few moments.

"The situation is bad." he said, "The helicopter overflew Dagenham and Romford as well as Hornchurch. Shopping centres have been gutted. There's furniture scattered around the gardens of private houses. They even spotted bodies in the streets. There're small groups of people in the fields including children. I'm ordering recces of Tilbury and Thamesport as well as Sheerness."

"How do you mean?" David asked.

"Tilbury and Thamesport are also container ports. If things go the way you expect then I may as well discover what resources are available." he explained, "I've sent a signal describing the situation and I'm waiting for a reply."

"What about that sailor's home?" David asked, "Did he find anyone?"

"They hovered over it." Commander Richards replied, "A couple of young men came out and looked. They saw someone in the street and it looked as if he had a gun. Ordinary Seaman Smith didn't recognise anyone. He's pretty cut up about it."

"Does he think that you could do more?" David asked.

"I'm not sure that's an appropriate question." Commander Richards replied with a frown, "It's not a good time for the crew to start questioning my orders."

"I don't know about that." David exclaimed, "The others might believe him more than you that a rescue is impossible and that you're going to have leave people to die."

"Including their families. God, what a mess."

David sat quietly glad that he did not have to make the decisions confronting Commander Richards.

There was little more that he could so he went back to the river-bus. Control of events was passing to Commander Richards and he was suffering from a reaction as he realised that the others could manage without him. He had got used to having a purpose in life and he felt empty now that it had gone.

He was not left alone for long before the same seaman approached him again, asking him to join Commander Richards. This time the Captain was thoughtful as he gestured David to a seat and offered him a whiskey.

"I've been ordered to Dover." he said, "They're reviving some contingency plans they had for World War Three. Dover Castle is now the Regional Command Centre for the Southern Area and I'm under their command. They're abandoning the cordons and I'm to rescue as many soldiers as possible. Do you have any thoughts on the matter?"

"I don't know Dover." David answered, "What's it like there?"

"It's a ferry port so there're lorries full of stores, if that's what you're thinking. There's good access roads for convoys and of course the Castle has always been used for this sort of thing."

"What? Hiding, believing that there'll be food to transport and fuel for the lorries?" David snapped, "How big is Dover? Will they be able to feed the inhabitants? What do you think that they want warships and troops for?"

"It comes back to feeding many short term or a few, long term, doesn't it?" Commander Richards said softly, "I've acknowledged that signal and signalled RCC Dover that I'm stockpiling food at a secure base and requested permission to continue the operation. I'm hoping that they'll see the sense in continuing and agree. It's a fudge but I'm not ready to openly defy orders yet."

"Fair enough." David said, "Would you have to pass Sheerness to get to Dover?"

"Of course." Commander Richards replied surprised at the question. To him it was elementary geography that Sheerness was in the Thames Estuary and so he would have to pass it to get out to sea and round the coast to Dover.

"Then you'll be obeying orders when you go there. The

problem will be when you stop."

David returned to the river-bus, looking exasperated as the seaman hurried after him once again. Again David was shown to the Captain's cabin. This time an army officer was also present.

"This is Major Davies." Captain Richards said by way of greeting, "This is Mr. Robson, Major. The Major was ordered to report here for transport to Dover."

Major Davies glared at him, "I don't think we need a civilian here. Orders apply to military personnel only."

"What's the situation, out there?" David asked, "Is everything organised? Is food being distributed to everyone who needs it? Can my lot return to London knowing everything's going to be all right?"

The Major slumped down in his seat.

"We were on our way to an exercise so we were ordered to clear the M25 through Essex then start on links to key routes." he said, "We abandoned our vehicles and marched. There were a couple of accidents on slip roads when the traffic lights went out. In other places it just started to tail back. When night fell people just abandoned their cars and tried walking. I think most headed for the nearest station hoping to catch a train. It took us a day to clear a mile of single lane when we were ordered to create the cordon.

"Luckily we had full field rations so we were OK but the civilians were getting desperate. Some hadn't had a drink for over a day. They were milling around on both sides of the cordon. Were we supposed to allow those already crossing the road to get through or push those on the outside back in? It didn't matter. There were no troops on either side of us so they could just go round. And this was just commuters on the motorway not London being emptied. Then we were ordered to report here for transport to Dover."

"So you've got working phones?" David asked.

"Radios." Major Davies corrected, "The phones are down. There's no civilian communications apart from C.B. and amateur radio."

"And what about the civilians when you left."

"We had to leave them. We went cross country and even in full pack we outran most of them."

There was a touch of pride in his voice as he boasted of his men's fitness but the horror of what he had done was still haunting him.

"You didn't try feeding them?" David asked.

"It was water they needed. God help me but if we'd tried to help them then my men would be going thirsty by now and it wouldn't have made any difference to that crowd."

"I thought the government was giving water supplies priority." Commander Richards said.

"Who knows?" Major Davies retorted angrily, "I can't believe what's happening. Some areas have already lost the mains supply, others are losing pressure."

"So it's not just vandalism?" David asked.

"I doubt it." Major Davies replied.

"David here, is convinced that we won't get a clear picture of the disaster for at least six months and that we should hold out somewhere for that long."

He paused, staring at Major Davies.

"Irrespective of our orders." he added, "I'm having contingency plans drawn up to salvage as much food as we can, store it in a defensible area and distribute as far as feasible. If Dover does establish control of the area then I shall obey orders, otherwise…"

He trailed off unwilling to admit to being ready to defy authority.

"Otherwise we're on our own." Major Davies finished, "And we must act on our own initiative."

"I'm going to wait here for as long as possible. My orders are to pick up any army units that get here so I can also justify waiting for stragglers. While we're waiting I'm loading a ferry with as much food as I can find. I'll make sure it includes bottled water."

Major Davies nodded.

"My men will help." he said, "How are you doing?"

"Better than I expected." Commander Richards replied, "These particular docks cater for roll-on-roll-off ferries. It's a case of opening each container then driving the ones we want onto a ferry that has just unloaded. We're jury rigging power from the ships to operate the cranes. Some crews stayed on board and they're helping. We can combine scratch crews to get one or two ships under way as soon as we're ready. I'm thinking that David might ferry a contingent of your troops down to Tilbury to secure the containers there."

Major Davies nodded, "It makes sense to me."

"And to me." David answered.

Major Davies looked annoyed but before he could say anything Commander Richards intervened.

"David understood the situation right from the start and got his people out of London with a viable plan to see them through the coming winter. For that reason alone, I value his opinions. I'm not sure that I like how he learnt to think so far outside the box but he does and I value his opinions as much as yours."

"So what are your recommendations?" Major Davies asked David. He was not prepared to apologise for his attitude but he was prepared to give David a chance to prove himself.

"Persuade Captain Richards to answer my question." David replied, "Do we feed a hundred people for one day or one person for a hundred days?"

"I'm only a Commander, not a Captain." he said, "I'm just Captain of this ship."

"And you're dodging the question again, Commander." David retorted, "In fact according to Major Davies, the question is, do we give water to a hundred…"

"Yes, Yes. I hear you." Commander Richards yelled angrily, "What am I supposed to say? We're going to let thousands of British subjects die without even trying to help them. It's the logical action but I'll never forgive myself if I do."

"Major Davies has already been in that position." David said quietly, "So he knows what it feels like and he still thought that there was a government to put things right later. It'll be worse for you because you know that any you leave will die."

"With David's permission, I'll send men down to Tilbury on his boat and set up a defensive perimeter. Perhaps some of his er, crew could start checking the containers."

David nodded, "It'll give them something to do. We'll need people who know how to set up these power supplies."

"The containers seem to be stored on a quay that is surrounded by water on three sides." Commander Richards said, "It should be easy to defend so perhaps you could tie up there as backup for the troops."

"As long as any food and water you use gets replaced." David said, "Remember, neither of you have to follow my plans so my lot needs to be able to go back to our original one."

The Major nodded, "That's fair."

"There's something else." David said, "You've arrested people on boats. What's the point. You're only going to have feed them and guard them. There's a woman on my boat who's under arrest. If she still wants to go, then I'm going to let her."

Commander Richards nodded, "We'll make some supplies available if they want to go. Will you speak to them and explain the situation. You've got a knack of saying how it is."

"OK but can someone ask Julie to bring Lily to me."

David was taken to where the yachtsmen were held. It comprised of a cafeteria on the ground floor with an area on the floor above that was used for sleeping. Sentries guarded it.

As soon as he entered he was almost mobbed by people desperate for news. Lily and Julie arrived shortly after. Fortunately the crowd was a little more willing to calm down on a policeman's instructions. She pointed to a table. David took the hint and jumped up on it.

"You all know the situation." he said matter of factly, "A solar flare's knocked out electricity. So far as we can tell the damage is worldwide. The power can't be repaired because there's not enough spares. We can't make any more spares because there's no power. Without power there's no water. The supply is failing fast. According to the doctor, what little natural water is available will be contaminated so there's going to be cholera, typhus and a lot of other nasty stuff.

"We don't believe we can put things back together again or save more than a handful of people. My boat was planning to hide for at least six months. If any of you can see out the winter then go for it. For the rest of you, we can give you some water but when you leave, you won't be allowed back."

"How long do you think it will take the Americans to get here?" someone asked.

"About a thousand years." David replied, "They relied on electricity more than we did. They're going to be harder hit than us. According to my experts we stand more chance of getting help from Afghanistan. It's backward enough to survive without electricity."

"So who are you and how come you're in charge?" another yachtsman asked, "You're a bit young aren't you?"

"I'm the guy that got my friends out of London without getting arrested." David replied, "I've also got the police on side, which is pretty amazing considering my record."

"You don't seem to be taking this very seriously, young man. Maybe we should wait for someone in charge."

"So far as civilians are concerned, he is in charge." Julie said, "His judgement has been spot on so far. People who ignored him have got others killed."

"You seem to be contemplating the end of civilisation as we know it." another said, "I put it to you that you're causing unnecessary alarm for your own ends. You've hinted at being some sort of criminal, I further put it to you that you intend looting in the confusion."

"Lily there is convinced that if she can get home to her father then she will be safe." David said, "She's already got one woman, a mother killed trying. I'm thinking of giving her enough food and water for the journey and chucking her out. Do you want to go with her? Her father's a judge, you sound like a lawyer so you should get on fine."

The lawyer smiled, "I accept your point but are you talking about the end of civilisation?"

It was the question that David desperately tried to avoid. He was not used to seeing beyond his immediate survival but now the question was out in the open again he found himself considering something almost beyond his imagination. He was far less certain as he prepared to answer.

"I've talked about fracture points and stuff and it's happening so fast." he almost whispered, "It seems more real every time I say it and yes, it's all gone and it's not coming back."

He left a shocked silence in the room.

"Rubbish." Lily snapped, "There's people like Daddy. They'll be organising things. I bet we'll be getting supplies any day now. You don't have to chuck me out as you so nicely put it. If I head out across country, I can make it. The masses don't know the country. They'll just stick to the roads and towns. Does anyone want to come with me? I bet we'll meet up with organised troops before we get very far anyway."

For some reason everyone turned back to David, expecting an argument from him.

"It's your lives." he said, "We'll just have fewer mouths to feed."

"And will you be able to feed everyone?" the lawyer asked.

"That's not the problem." David said, "We need to obtain drinking water first."

"I was planning on wintering in the South of France." the lawyer said, "I may continue with that plan. My boat was already stocked for the journey. What do you think?"

"It's as good a plan as any." David replied, "Can you sail across the ocean without any radio help?"

"It's the English Channel and the Bay of Biscay. That's not ocean but it's still a good point. The weather would be the biggest danger. However, if I leave now the odds would be in my favour. What do you say, dear?"

He turned to a woman standing beside him who nodded.

"I'll get someone to take you out to your boat." David said, "Good luck."

"And to you, young man. Please do not be offended but I look forward to prosecuting you when the courts reopen. You're probably right though and I think that I may end my days fishing from my boat and selling my catch in exchange for water from some African village well."

David smiled, "I'd have an interesting defence though. Let's hope we do meet in court."

"There's a village I know in Scotland." another said, "I think that they'll manage without electricity. Would you stock me for the journey?"

"If we've got water for a week then we'll give you a week's supply, but no more." David said, "Apart from that, good luck to you as well."

David jumped down from the table. He was glad to see that most understood what their options were, and were planning their next move. As David made his way to the door, he was blocked by an elderly man. He was not particularly big or threatening but there was something commanding about him.

"I'm Professor Jacobsen." he said, "I'm a naturalist. Most of my work has been in the Amazon but I got my love of the subject from the English countryside. I know you don't need my help now but what of the future?"

"If you're prepared to stay for a few days then I'll talk to you." David said, "The navy boys keep talking about contingency plans.

Can you do something like that?"

"I should think so." he said, "I'd like to work on my boat. It'll be quieter but I was heading for Chatham Marina to stock up there."

"OK." David said, "I'm going to see Commander Richards. Let's see what he says."

David was exhausted when he entered the Commander's cabin. He could scarcely believe that it was only mid afternoon. Neither Commander Richards nor Major Davies looked much better. Although they did not realise it, they were all in shock, overwhelmed by events.

Professor Jacobsen actually provided some relief. He talked briefly of what wild edible plants grew and discussed the chances of planting wheat and barley. For once, the future seemed brighter with a little hope.

"What about meat?" Major Davies asked.

"Animals aren't going to fare much better than humans. Dairy cattle haven't been milked for three days. I'm not sure what that's going to do to them. Farmers aren't going to be able milk them all by hand though they could drink the milk. Organic farms might fare better but an awful lot is dependent on technology I don't know what will happen."

A lot of animals will go wild so hunting may be an option but when it comes to farming, it takes twenty times the land to produce the equivalent quantity of food through meat. We'll have the space. It's working it that will be the problem. Rats and mice should be plentiful in the first few years though. I believe that they're quite nutritious."

"Gladys reckons the milk might last a few more days." David said, "Then it's black tea and coffee. I wonder how soon we could start trading with the farmers?"

"I don't want to rush you, David." Commander Richards said, "But you should leave now if we're going to secure Tilbury by nightfall."

"What do you say?" David asked, "Aye, aye, sir? I'm on my way."

David was glad to finally get back to the river-bus. He gathered the others together and briefed them on what was happening. The boys were more excited than anything. Oliver hugged him and held him as if he'd been gone for days. Lieutenant

Scales and Tom were still discussing plans to occupy Sheerness docks.

"It sounds as if you've started without us." Tom retorted, "Still maybe we should move fast and we've got a military escort past the cordon. Well done."

David grinned before turning to Julie.

"Things are breaking up fast. Do you want to stay with us?"

"I'll stay as long as you've got the army and navy on side." she grinned before becoming serious, "I've got no response on my radio but I could be out of range. I should report to the nearest police station but is it still operational? My orders were to keep an eye on you and it's still the most sensible plan."

While Tom headed for the wheelhouse to start the engines, David found an empty table to sit quietly. Jake and Rory still acted as lookouts and it was Jake who informed him that a soldier wanted to see him. Major Davies had sent a platoon of soldiers under the command of a young lieutenant whose orders were to place himself under David's command. Commander Richards had also sent a squad of his own men.

Normally no officer would hand over command to a civilian like that but Major Davies was as scared as the rest. He was also as concerned for his family as everyone else. He had seen the chaos and would have nightmares for many years thinking about refusing water to so many desperate people. Only David seemed to think that he was right so he needed David to prove himself worth listening to.

The sailors knew that David had persuaded their Captain to try a rescue of one of their shipmate's family so he was already popular with them. David was unaware of any of it. He just found himself as busy as ever.

The Army lieutenant was as keen as his major to have someone around who knew what to do but he resented having to obey such a young, obviously inexperienced civilian.

It did not help when David simply sent Jake to tell him to get everyone on board then for him to come down to the saloon.

David was just getting to used to a formal handshake rather than a non-committal 'hi' when meeting someone for the first time so his greeting was a little awkward. Gladys appeared with a tray of tea and biscuits so the lieutenant relaxed a little.

"I take it you want to plan everything like a military

operation." David said, pausing then adding with a grin added, "I suppose it is a military operation so what do you want to do?"

"You're in charge so you tell me." the lieutenant snapped, "You're the expert."

"I want to grab enough food and water to supply as many as people as possible for six months." David replied calmly, "After six months I don't know but my guess is that there'll be a few million dead, including my family and yours. What's left will be back to farming or hunting. When you land at Tilbury do you intend killing anyone you find there or feeding them?"

David had found that the best way of dealing with people was to make them tackle the moral dilemmas they faced. It was a good trick because like the question he had just asked the Lieutenant, they were usually unanswerable.

"I don't know." the lieutenant replied though a little less belligerently, "Again, you're in charge. What are your orders?"

"Some of them will just be looters." David replied, "Some might be trying to set up their own scheme. Others may want to help and we could do with it."

"And?" the Lieutenant asked.

"Don't let anything go to waste." David replied, "You might have to shoot someone who can't accept that but I'm not sure that we should fight anyone with a workable plan."

"You mean you don't know?" the Lieutenant asked triumphantly.

"No I don't." David said angrily, "What I do know is that you're trying to get one over on me instead of figuring out how to get supplies. I hope you remember how good that feels when your troops are starving."

The lieutenant was silent for a time. David was right and had got the measure of him. Maybe he did know what he was doing.

"I'm sorry, sir." the lieutenant said, "I've got photos from the helicopter recce. I suggest we send an advanced guard in the smaller boats to secure a small area of the dock where we can tie up then fan out."

"You're the expert, so it's up to you." David replied.

"What do we do about civilians on the dock?" the lieutenant asked.

"We've had one woman on board that's already got two people

killed and a third injured. I've put her ashore so she can't do any more harm. She was one of four people who tried raiding this boat for food. The other three are still with us and the two guys will be helping you. We were lucky and able to get more rations to cover them. I don't know if I'm answering your question but if we can look after them for six months then we may as well do so."

"If things stay bad, what happens then?" the Lieutenant asked.

"Pray that we've learnt to become water diviners, farmers and hunters." David replied grimly.

"So all we're doing is getting ourselves a breathing space?" the Lieutenant asked.

David nodded.

"Without clean water, people are going to start dying in a few days." he said, "It's cold enough for frost at night. That'll take care of a few more, then the food will start running out. We need to be clear of the towns by then. With no heating, how many of those left will survive the Winter? Once Spring comes there won't be many left and if you can put up with the stink, we'll be able to scavenge the cities for our own stuff."

"My wife's in Devon. She's visiting her parents." the lieutenant almost sobbed, "We've only been married six months."

"What are your chances of meeting up again?" David asked as gently as he could then waiting, expecting, almost demanding a reply.

"We'd both make our way to Aldershot." the lieutenant replied, "I could try heading along the M25. I'd meet everyone escaping London crossing it and if I carried supplies then I'd be a target. I couldn't fight them all off. Brianna would have to make her way up the A-roads and go through every town and village."

"So what are your chances?" David persisted.

"I know what the fucking chances are." the Lieutenant yelled, "It doesn't stop me thinking I should try."

"See what you can do about keeping your men's mobiles charged up." David said, "If they've got email addresses give them to the kids. They've got laptops and if the Internet does start working then they can monitor all the addresses. It's not much but it might make your men feel better if something is being done, but for now, can we go back to getting our supplies together?"

"My name's Jack Riley." the Lieutenant said, "Would you like to come along with us?"

David guessed that Lieutenant Riley was trying to make amends for his behaviour.

"No." David replied, "I'd only get in the way and I can't believe that you want a civilian hanging around."

Jack Riley grinned, "Normally I wouldn't but this is way outside my training. I'm still not sure what I should do about scavengers we find."

"I'll stay with the river-bus." David said, "Just secure a dock for us and I'll join you as soon as we arrive. If you're attacked, then you'll have to fire back. Just don't turn it into a massacre."

Jack nodded.

The two work boats set off, each with half a dozen soldiers on board. Tom let the river-bus follow about a mile behind. The top deck was full of the remaining soldiers and a group of sailors. The children were rushing excitedly around and some soldiers found their excitement infectious and were happily chatting to them.

The sergeant in charge seemed a little annoyed when David approached him.

"We should have put you civilians ashore." he snapped, "Can't you keep those kids under control?"

"No." David snapped back, "Their parents are missing. Emma saw her mother killed. They've been shot at yet they do their share of lookout duty and other work. If you're short of radios then Jake and Rory will take messages for you. For now, they can have some fun."

The sergeant glowered at him.

"We'll have National Service back before this lot's finished. Then you'll all learn how to behave."

"Let's hope things stay that well organised." David replied grimly, "In the meantime, we're all trying to survive so that puts us on the same side."

The sergeant continued to stare angrily at him. David headed for the wheelhouse, beckoning Rory to follow him. Jake naturally tagged along while Oliver continued an earnest conversation with an amused young soldier.

Emma was still in shock and stayed close to her brother but she felt the safest knowing where Gladys and Jessica were. She kept an eye on the stairs to the saloon ready to bolt to safety. There was something soothing about their talk of babies, cooking and other domestic chores.

Julie on the other hand was as daunting as the men.

"Take these binoculars and watch the other boats." David said, "Don't disturb Tom unless something seems to be wrong. If you do see something, then one of you come and fetch me and the sergeant."

The two boys nodded solemnly.

The river zigzagged between Dartford and Tilbury. They were on the second leg coming up to the final bend to the right. The boys were already scanning the shore looking for the boats and shouted delightedly as they spotted them. They were beached on a muddy embankment close to the main container handling area and the soldiers were already scrambling over the seawall that topped it. David tensed, waiting for the sounds of gunfire but it remained quiet.

The river-bus continued it's cautious approach. Suddenly the soldiers appeared again. They were on the main quay where the largest container ships tied up. It was still quiet and they seemed relaxed. David took the binoculars to study the docks. There was a group of civilians standing with their hands above their heads. As he watched, a couple more soldiers appeared from behind a barrier following four more civilians who were placed with rest.

David was relieved that no one had been hurt so far. He glanced at the sergeant who seemed oblivious to the developing scene. David frowned. The sergeant was not really oblivious to it all, he was just not trying to understand it. He ordered his men to get ready to provide covering fire and they lined the railings to one side and the front ready to open up. It was probably the right thing to do but David was uneasy.

The people already captured were less of a threat than a counter-attack from beyond the containers. He wanted to ask the Sergeant about it but he thought the soldier would resent it.

They edged towards the quay. Lieutenant Riley turned and waved to them, beckoning them in to tie up alongside a ladder. The soldiers scrambled ashore, taking up positions around the landing area. Jack Riley saw David watching and beckoned him up as well. As David headed for the Lieutenant, he sent for one of the prisoners who introduced himself rather pompously as Mr. Smith.

There's always one, David laughed to himself.

"You've no right arresting us." he said, "I shall lodge an official complaint."

"Who with?" David asked.

Mr. Smith glared at him, "The police of course. This is private property and the army has no jurisdiction here."

"Ignoring Martial Law for the moment," David said, "can you even find a policeman who's still on duty?"

Mr. Smith slumped, defeated, "So what do you intend to do?"

"I assume you're looking for food." David replied, "So are we. We want to keep as many people alive as possible until next spring."

"There's not enough food to supply everyone that long." Mr. Smith exclaimed, "It won't work, people are already hungry and the water supply pressure seems to be dropping. It's getting bad."

"We're not trying to save everyone." David said sadly, "We're trying to save as many as we can. How much water do you have left?"

"I don't know." Mr. Smith replied, "The government said that it was going to keep the water mains on so it's probably only a temporary problem."

"I doubt it." David said, "You need to arrange clean water and a sewerage system. How many people can you handle?"

"I don't know." Mr. Smith cried, "There are women and children depending on us. We can't just abandon them."

"Look, I keep having this conversation and I don't like it any more now than I did the first time." David snapped, "Millions are going to die. Now the water's failing, most will die of thirst, then they'll start getting diseases from drinking dirty water, and when winter comes what's left will freeze to death. What's left of the Government is holed up in a nuclear bunker at Dover."

He ran over to the quayside and saw the children on the deck watching events.

"Someone, fetch a radio will you please," he called out before returning to the others, "Let's listen to the hourly announcement and see what's happening."

It was Jake, glad to have a little responsibility, who proudly presented the radio to David. David tried tuning in but there was just static. He tried other stations but there was nothing.

"Can you radio Commander Richards, please." David asked Lieutenant Riley, "Maybe he can learn something from the Regional Command Centre."

Jack nodded and hurried off.

"How come you're in charge." Mr. Smith asked.

David noted some condescension in his voice but let it pass.

"Oh I'm just a thief who hated everyone telling me what to do." David replied mischievously, "I could talk my way out of trouble because I knew the system. When those stupid announcements started, I knew it was all bull."

Mr. Smith just looked at David, uncertain how to respond. Like others who had met him, he had the uncanny feeling that David knew what he was talking about. He did not want to believe him though. He could cope with a temporary glitch but David was talking about the complete destruction of his world.

"The Government knows what it's doing." Mr. Smith snapped, "It's obvious it's going to take time and it certainly doesn't need a yobbo like you causing trouble."

David shrugged.

"Either the water comes back on in the next couple of days or it doesn't. If it does then you'll need to find food for everyone for a couple of weeks. If you start getting food supplies in by then, all you've got to do is keep them warm. So how many can you keep alive through the winter?"

"It's only October." Mr. Smith exclaimed, "There's time."

"Only if you're right." David retorted, just as angrily, "What happens if they get it wrong and the delays get longer or are you saying the Government never gets it wrong?"

The argument stopped as Lieutenant Riley returned.

"We've orders to take all the food to Dover." he said, "We're also to commandeer all water supplies that can be transported. We're to treat all civilians as disposable."

"What does that mean?" David and Mr. Smith asked, almost in unison.

"Commander Richards is seeking clarification but it sounds as if we're to shoot the lot of you if you try to stop us taking everything."

"This is Essex." Mr. Smith said desperately, "Dover would only have jurisdiction over Kent. Where's our Regional Command Centre?"

"It's a legal nicety." Lieutenant Riley grinned before becoming serious again, "I don't think it matters though. David, Commander Richards would like your estimate of the situation. I'd like to hear as well."

David thought for a moment. They were not asking for his advice. They were seeking confirmation that things were still getting bad. His only real ability had been to do what he had always done. Distrust those in authority. Conversely, he felt better that it was Commander Richards and Major Davies who had the real authority for now but it was still wearing constantly seeing the bleak side of everything.

"We should stay here for a week." he said, "Get the food supplies organised and see what happens. I learnt about cholera at school on one of those Third World gigs. I reckon we'll be seeing it here by then."

He paused, looking at Mr. Smith, "If I'm right of course. In which case we'll also be able to start estimating how many are dying of thirst."

"You're a cold one." Mr. Smith exclaimed, "You just don't seem to care do you? I suppose that's life on the streets for you."

For once, it became too much for David and his anger and frustration welled up inside him. As tears filled his eyes, he swung a punch at Mr. Smith. Luckily Jack saw it and grabbed his arm.

"Easy." the Lieutenant said, "I agree with you in one way, Mr. Smith. It's not easy knowing that the only person who understands this situation is some street punk. Some of my men have been asking when the Americans will get here. They're probably worse hit than we are. The only countries that can help will be Third World ones that did not rely on electricity and telecommunications. From what I hear David is predicting the end of civilisation as we know it and he's planning a new one. Isn't that right David."

David was still angry and close to tears.

"I don't want to have this conversation again." he sobbed, "It's killing me knowing I can't help my family. All I hear about is other people's families. Of course, I care but what can I do."

"Easy David." Lieutenant Riley said, "I'm not trying to insult you but if you'd chosen to stay in London then you'd be running one of those gangs by now. There's something of a gang attitude in you in that you look after your own and to hell with the rest."

"Isn't that what the government's doing at Dover?" David exclaimed, "But does it matter? If you want to prove how superior you all are then go ahead start giving food to everyone and hope the government gets here in time. My lot will carry on down stream and sit it out during the winter as we planned."

"I'm sorry." Mr. Smith said, "You're right. There's not enough food or water. I often wondered how the crew of Titanic felt knowing that there were not enough seats in the lifeboats. Now I know and I wish I didn't."

"We need to know how much water we can produce and use the figure to bring a number of people onto the quay." David said, "Check out all the ships in dock and see how they get fresh water."

"What about a 'children only' policy?" Mr. Smith asked.

"We'll still have to limit numbers." David replied, "It's not going to be easy, whatever we decide. I'm going back to the river-bus and tell my lot what's happening. I suggest you two let your own guys know what's going on. Lieutenant Riley's in charge so I guess it's down to him to figure out what to do."

"If you've got any plans then I'd like to hear them." Jack replied, "I think I'm about to commit mutiny by ignoring Dover's orders so listening to a civilian is a minor problem."

David turned to Mr. Smith, waiting.

"I was unnecessarily rude to you. Again, I apologise." Mr. Smith said, "In the light of what I've heard you're right and we've got to plan for the worst. What do you want me to do."

"If anyone leaves this dock then they can't come back." David said, "We need a quarantine area just beyond it. When diseases start, we'll have to hold people there. We'll need volunteers to organise it on the outside. Think about it."

Mr. Smith swallowed nervously and nodded. The scavengers who had been rounded up consisted of several men, women and three children. Whatever else happened he was not going to let the children leave the dock. He was a solicitor, living in a modest detached house overlooking the river on the outskirts of Tilbury. He was a widower and his only son lived in America.

The town was not so small that everybody knew everyone else but it was normal to meet someone you knew when you went out. Mr. Smith had been part of a group who had organised a rationing system. Although it stayed strictly within the guidelines in the radio announcements, it had been fairly done and by and large had been successful though with the situation obviously deteriorating panic was setting in.

Mr. Smith was on the quay that day because the ration organisers were beginning to accept that they were going to have to take more drastic steps. Like the military and naval officers that David had talked to he had been unwilling to think about the full consequences of the unfolding disaster. Neither was he willing to believe that the Government had all but vanished.

The failing water supply had jolted him. One or two residents who worked away, had managed to get home and they had talked of bodies in the fields and people desperately drinking from ditches. Many people seemed unable to take in what was happening and stayed in their homes waiting for the government to sort it out. Commuters trudged along the main routes out of cities trying to get home. So far, few refugees had reached Tilbury but the numbers were increasing.

As Mr. Smith considered David's remarks so the notion that he would soon be dead took deeper root. He was not a brave man, the future scared him and leaving the relative safety of the quay terrified him. However, organising the quarantine area was something he understood and saving just one life would give his own life meaning.

"If I leave now, perhaps I can take some sort of radio with me." Mr. Smith said, looking at David, "I'll try to tell people what's happening."

David turned to Lieutenant Riley uncertain what to say.

"You need to see Major Davies." Jack said, "You can't make these decisions on your own. I'll detail a couple of sailors to take you."

"It's OK. I can manage one of those work boats." David replied.

"Senior officers are transported." Lieutenant Riley grinned, "You've got a lot of the responsibility so enjoy the perks."

"Thanks." David said, "But you're all going to get tired of talking to me. I'll be back to just being a deadbeat loser then."

"The best scenario is that we still have a functional government and things will start getting better." Jack said, "We'll all feel a bit stupid for listening to you and enjoy watching that police woman arrest you. For now, you're our expert so enjoy it."

"OK, in that case, I'd like Mr. Smith to come with me."

David went to the river-bus to tell the others what was happening then allowed himself to be ferried to the frigate.

"I've been thinking about it ever since that stupid order not to use the toilets." David said, "Without water we're fucked."

"Take it easy." Commander Richards said quietly, "I agree with you. Water is the key. Major Davies and I are under orders to report to Dover after commandeering as much food as possible. I assume the castle's got wells they can use."

"So what do you intend doing?" David asked.

Commander Richards stared at him, steadily without blinking.

"You've probably heard that we've orders to consider the civilian population as disposable. From the signals we've intercepted Dover is going to be little more than an armed camp. The docks are not as defensible as these."

"Exactly. We're set up so that we can retreat onto ships and move away." Major Davies interrupted, "You've got politicians there still thinking in terms of running a government. The castle's too far from the docks."

"I'm going to allow as many children as we can handle onto the quays." Commander Richards said, "I'm willing to disobey orders that far. Beyond that, we'll have to wait and see. Start with five year olds then raise the age until we've reached our quota."

"Why not younger?" David asked.

"Because they'll need their mothers and that reduces the number of children we can take."

"Set up a children's area just off the quay." David said, "We'll all ration our water so that there's as much as possible to spare and issue it there. That way, a few of the parents can organise it."

"Good idea. Mr. Smith, will you arrange it, please.?"

Mr. Smith nodded, "I'll head back now. The sooner we start doing something the less likely it is that people will panic."

He stood up and offered his hand to David.

"Good luck, young man." he said, "I don't think that I'm going to live to see the worst of this but you're going to endure it all."

With that he was gone leaving the others in thoughtful silence.

"Comments?" Commander Richards asked, "David?"

"Are there still places with wells?" he asked thoughtfully, "Could we find them and distribute water that way?"

"It's a thought." Commander Richards replied, "But without a sewerage system how quickly would they become contaminated?"

"It would also mean scattering troops." Major Davies added,

"We're stretched as it is."

"How about seeing if we can find any more of the crew's families?" David asked.

"No one complained about the last trip and we could do with getting a better picture of what's happening but it's not going to solve the water supply though."

"No, but we're talking about how many people we'll be turning away. I was just thinking of people we could save for a bit."

"Do you want to check on your mother?" Major Davies asked.

Tears filled David's eyes.

"We land in a park, fight our way through the gangs to the flats, get up to the fifth floor then come back again." he sobbed, "Of course I want to but I can't, can I?"

"If it's any consolation, you've saved more lives than anyone else." Commander Richards said, "You saw the true situation and managed to convince the rest of us. Even children at Tilbury will live because of your foresight."

He hesitated for a moment, "I'm ordering a flight to Dover at first light. If there's any sort of organisation, then I'm obeying orders. If any of the Navy command centres are still functional, then again I'll obey their orders. However, without a national government I doubt whether they are. If I can't find any evidence of a planned response to this situation then I intend saving as many people as I can. If that happens then I'll regard David as the senior civilian official."

He grinned, "It's a sobering thought but it could make you the last British Government."

"It makes me want to get drunk not sober. Two things. You should move down river to the other side of the bridge. I don't suppose anyone's got a drone with a camera, have they? It might be an idea to check on what anyone's doing up there. The other thing is, could I have a word with O.S. Smith please."

Night 4

A little later David was welcoming O.S. Smith aboard the river-bus. It was dusk and the two young men sat on the deck drinking an inevitable cup of tea freshly brewed by Gladys.

"So what did you make of it?" David asked, "Could we have rescued your family?"

O.S. Smith struggled to keep control, "No sir, Cherie was probably at work or stuck on a train somewhere. Mum's house was empty. She usually collects Ashley from school. God knows where they are."

"What about one of those movies?" David asked, "You know, you head off and nothing stops you until you've found your family."

"You didn't, sir. You knew it was impossible. Mum and Ashley might be trying to make it to one of my brothers or sisters. It would take weeks to find all of them."

"Call me David. Commander Richards won't like me asking this but what about the rest of the crew? How many want to try to make it home?"

"There're a few hotheads. The rest like the idea of getting a proper base. We're all keeping our phones and computers charged up like you suggested."

"So everyone's going to keep on obeying orders?" David asked.

O.S. Smith nodded, "I reckon so. At least for now. You and the Captain seem to know what you're doing."

"OK! All them officer types still think in the old ways. I need to know if it starts going wrong." David smiled, "Don't worry. I'm not planning a mutiny. I need to know when to start talking to Commander Richards."

"I understand, sir." O.S. Smith replied.

David was exhausted. His mind was buzzing round in circles trying to figure out what to do. When Gladys asked him if he wanted another cup of tea he could not make up his mind. Concerned she spoke to Tom.

"It's probably beginning to sink in." Tom said, "I bet he saw it as a game at first. You know, trying to outwit the authorities or something. Get him to rest."

Tom was beginning to feel the same way. Only the children still saw it as an adventure. They might be worried about their families but the adults would sort it and when their parents phoned they would be able to tell them all about it."

The women were also feeling the effects of post traumatic stress and shock. However, there was a comforting and familiar domesticity that helped everyone. Julie might be cleaning her gun but she could cheerfully chat to Gladys and Jessica about the baby. Gladys was still the old fashioned housewife. Increasingly the saloon was her domain, putting anyone with nothing better to do, to clean and help prepare meals.

Oliver was worried that David looked so tired. He stayed close by, ready to run any little errand for David and settling down to sleep with him again. The next morning David was left to sleep until Commander Richards sent for him again.

Day 5

As he sat down to breakfast David noticed some strange children in the cabin, watching him, eventually recognising them as the children on the dock the previous afternoon.

"Lieutenant Riley sent them over." Gladys said, "We can't send them away, can we."

Gladys was not asking but stating a fact. She still needed David's approval but she was prepared to stand her ground and argue with him.

One of the strangers was a youth of about sixteen. David called him over.

"Have you had your breakfast." he asked.

"Yeah. The old girl cooked us something."

"Her name is Gladys." David said sternly, "Disrespect her and you'll be chucked off. Do you know how bad things are?"

"Yeah. Old man, I mean Mr. Smith told us all about it. I wanted to help Mum and Dad but Dad told me stay here. He and Mr. Smith reckon I've got a better chance. I ought to find my girlfriend though."

"The rule is if you leave, you don't come back." David said, "Help us to organise the supplies. It's the best way of helping her."

"So everyone says." the youth exclaimed, "But I feel as if I'm running out on them."

"I know what you mean." David said, "I keep thinking of those films where they rush off and rescue their families. I should be doing that. The worse things get the more I feel as if I'm running out on them. It must be harder for you, you like your family."

David paused as the boy stared in surprise then laughed.

David continued, "I'm serious. I bet my cousins have stocked their place full of TVs and laptops. They wouldn't think of stockpiling food or water. Those other kids over there will be thinking the same as you. Their parents are waiting just off the quay. You go running off and they're likely to follow. Sorry but you've got to choose between them and your girlfriend. Just remember you won't be able to help anyone if you're dying of thirst."

The boy nodded, "Yeah. It is safer here, isn't it? It still feels as if I'm hiding though."

"None of us feel good about it." David said, "Figure out how to get her enough water and heating for the winter. Oh and make sure it doesn't get nicked. If you can do that then I'll help you but I've got to go now."

"There's been some sort of battle in Dover." Commander Richards said when David arrived, "A convoy was set alight and there are bodies in the neighbouring streets. They look as if they were shot or hit with grenades."

"What about the castle?" David asked.

There was no radio contact with the helicopter. Maybe they didn't have the right frequencies. Troops waved and cheered as if it was a rescue and the helicopter didn't risk landing."

The Captain was badly shaken. He was white faced and his hands seemed to be trembling, looking twenty years older. He stared helplessly at David.

"What are we going to do?" he asked helplessly.

David was just as shocked, alarmed at the captain's collapse.

"I don't know." he whispered, "Supposing we'd been wiped out in a nuclear attack what would your orders be then?"

Commander Richards shrugged, "All the planning assumed that there would be some semblance of control. It seems to have all gone in a few days."

"Yes but the navy's got command centres hasn't it?" David persisted, "How come they're gone? Surely they were designed to resist an attack?"

"We're supposed to be under Dover's command." Commander Richards snapped, "Because of you I disobeyed those orders. When they do re-establish contact, I'll face court martial."

He slumped forward, resting his head in his hands.

"I'm sorry. That was uncalled for. My guess is this. They probably got warnings of the flare and even shut down some systems to protect them. However, how do you assess a completely new threat? Yes I know that they understood in theory but I'm talking about turning the theory into massive practice at extremely short notice. Key personnel may have been sent on leave until it was over. You know, they'd have nothing to do then afterwards they'd be working all hours to repair the damage."

"There are probably all sorts of variations to that scenario."

Major Davies said, "They all boil down to not being ready. I can't believe it's all gone in a few days, either."

He looked as ill and haggard as Commander Richards.

"What do we do, Mr. Robson?" Major Davies asked.

The sudden politeness startled David but Commander Richards was looking at him as well.

"What we've already planned except that I'm beginning to think that we should stay here instead of moving to Sheerness." David said, "What are you going to tell the crew and the soldiers?"

"As little as possible." Commander Richards said, "There's no point in alarming them more than we have to."

"I don't think that's a good idea." David said, "It's bad enough for us and we only talk about it. What about the ones who're going to keep desperate parents from feeding their kids?"

"Major Davies?" Commander Richards asked.

"My soldiers were ready to fight for Queen and Country." he replied, "What does it mean now?"

They sat in silence until Major Davies added, "Do what you think is right, Mr. Robson."

David glared angrily at him, "Don't fucking dump it all on me, you wanker. I can still take the river-bus down to the Medway. I don't need your shit."

Commander Richards shuddered then straightened up.

"Gentlemen, like it or not we share the authority so let's not bicker." he said, "David, you are right. You can leave whenever you want to. However, I would like you to stay. You are the elected civilian leader and in command of the civilian population. I was only partly joking earlier. Military services serve the civilian administration. I'm not sure what it all means now but at least it's a command structure I understand."

"Commander, there is no command structure." David said, "We're all trying to make sense of this and it's impossible. I'm not an elected anything. If the government's gone, then you're not even a commander. You may as well call yourself Admiral and give yourself the Victoria Cross. How about you Major? Do want to be a general or something?"

"Then how do we maintain discipline?" Major Davies asked.

"Why do you think we should?" David asked.

"Because we'll all probably die if we don't." Major Davies

exclaimed, "If we keep some sort of order then we'll be able to save lives."

"I agree." David said, "It's all we've got. It's why we should stay. How do we abandon all those people to go to Sheerness and tell another load of people that we can't help them?"

"Do you have any ideas?" Commander Richards asked.

"Tom and Lieutenant Scales should have the figures, but we'll still base our plans on how many we can save until the spring. I've got some crazy ideas. We take power from any ship we can, then run lines to the town and we tell them to plug in as many freezers as they can. A guy was telling me that they tried to make some hooch inside. They couldn't make a still so they tried freezing it. As it froze water formed a slush because it froze first. What was left was spirit. I think they were caught before they tried it but if the Thames is a bit cleaner than ditch water, would the ice be drinkable?" Or would it be easier to make stills?"

"It's a thought." Commander Richards said, "Anything else?"

"I've heard of edible tubers." David said, "But I'm a city boy. I don't know what they are. Are there any around and could anything be planted that would grow quickly?"

"You're talking about collecting wild food." Major Davies said, "Maybe Professor Jacobsen would help."

Both Major Davies and Commander Richards looked more cheerful as they considered the possibilities. David still felt as if everyone depended on him. He listened to the conversation but he was spent. As quickly as he could he left the officers to sort out details and headed for the river-bus.

It had become a refuge for him. Oliver immediately hurried over to greet and hug him while Gladys was ready with a 'nice cup of tea'. He would have preferred a beer but they were bottled and not perishable. Milk was, so tea and coffee was all that was on offer.

"Commander Richards should be in charge," he complained to Gladys, "but he's relying on me."

"He's highly trained and probably a brilliant seaman." Gladys said, "Everything he's relied on in the past is gone and he's probably in shock. I saw a programme about Titanic. It reckoned that its captain was affected the same way."

"You're the second person to have mentioned the Titanic." David exclaimed, "It's not the same."

"No it's not." Gladys agreed, "This is far worse. You're used to defying the world. The captain is used to being part of it."

How come, you're so calm?"

"Maybe because what I understand is still useful." Gladys replied, "If I was back home, I wonder how I'd be feeling by now."

"I'm just as scared as everyone else." David said. Briefly he felt embarrassed at admitting such a thing in front of Oliver and Gladys but Oliver hugged him.

"You don't act scared." he said, "You're trying to save us."

"He's right." Gladys said, "Only a fool wouldn't be scared at the moment."

"Yes but I shouldn't be in charge should I?"

"Probably not." Gladys agreed, "But it all seems to come down to this. You're not only willing to break the old rules and you're also willing to make new ones. What do you think is the most important job now?"

"Ollie, take the boat and take a message to Captain Richards." David said, "Tell him that I'm going to tell as many people as possible what's happening. I'm going to find Lieutenant Riley and tell him to set up a sound system. I want it relayed to the crews and everyone else who can hear. Do you understand?"

Oliver nodded, "Shall I see if it can be broadcast on the radio."

"No. I want radio silence. People outside of Tilbury might hear it. I don't want people rushing here thinking that they'll be saved."

"Yes sir." Oliver said then blushed, "You sounded like a teacher then."

"Tell me what you have to say."

Oliver repeated the message and left. David climbed up onto the quay to find Lieutenant Riley who looked relieved to see him.

"Those warehouses make a natural boundary. We've shifted containers to fill gaps and I've disposed troops to cover the area beyond. Crowds have been gathering. They yell a bit but they've done nothing so far. They're still using booze in the shops and pubs so we'll be getting a few drunks later."

David explained the speaker system he wanted.

"Set a microphone on a container opposite the biggest crowd." he said.

"That might be risky." Lieutenant Riley said, "Someone might take a pot shot at you."

"It might be easier if they did." David exclaimed angrily, "Someone else could take over then."

"Easy sir." the lieutenant said quietly, "You'll worry the troops if you talk like that. I'll get the PA set up."

David nodded, thinking about what he was going to say. *Street gang or government,* he thought, *If the leader doesn't sound strong then someone will be after him.*

He waited quietly until everything was ready. Oliver returned and ran over to him.

David grinned, "Now let's hope I don't get stage fright."

"Everyone does." Oliver said, "Our drama teacher said that even famous actors could be sick before going on."

He looked sad, "I wonder how they're all doing? They haven't got you."

"Listen Ollie." David said sharply, "I shouldn't be in charge. If you see a chance to get away, take it. I might kill you all."

"No you won't." Oliver said firmly, "I know I could die but what would I be doing in London? I've done better with you."

Despite Oliver's encouragement, David could not shake off the feeling of hopelessness he had. He felt numb and detached as Lieutenant Riley came for him. If the lieutenant had said that the firing squad was ready for him instead of the PA he would felt just as unconcerned.

He climbed the ladder onto the container feeling as if he was climbing the scaffold. He looked around seeing a couple of speakers. Looking across the clear space he saw a crowd milling around behind a line of cars that were obviously acting as a boundary wall. David took the microphone being offered to him, turning to the crowd.

"Will the crowd in front of me raise your hand if you can hear me." he said.

Hands obligingly shot up.

"Good from now on, I'm going to give you a daily report." he continued, "Without radio this is the easiest way of doing it. So here is the news.

"People have compared this situation to the Titanic. We don't have enough lifeboats and most of us are going to die. We can give out the water we've got but the quicker it's gone, the quicker we all die. We can hoard all the water we've got, sail from the docks and leave you to it. We'll live and you won't die much quicker."

He paused, "What we intend to do is take in as many of your children as we can keep alive until Spring. We expect that there will still be enough food to scavenge from the towns while we plant crops and search out wells. We can give you power from the ships so that you can obtain your own fresh water. If we do that then you will have the same problem as us. Who do you keep alive and for how long? Try to boil any water you drink. There's a strong risk of typhus, dysentery and cholera. We think that this will cause the most deaths."

He paused again letting everyone consider the implications, "We discussed this with a Mr. Smith yesterday but I don't see him today. He should already be arranging for the children. Will you try to find him, please?"

He thought about the government broadcasts repeating the important parts, "I repeat, we will try to save as many children as possible. Save means supplying water and food for the foreseeable future. If you can come up with your own plans, then we will help. For now, Mr. Smith should have started the organisation on your side. What happened to him?"

He lowered the microphone then climbed back down the ladder

As his feet touched the ground he began shaking, almost collapsing. Oliver leapt forward to grab him, closely followed by Lieutenant Riley. Sentries guarding the perimeter looked worriedly on. David was talking to them as much as anyone and he still had the reputation of knowing what he was doing.

"Take some long slow deep breaths. It's some sort of stress reaction." Lieutenant Riley said, "I'll get you to the sick bay."

David shook his head and, as he tried the breathing exercise he began to feel better.

"Just for once I'd like one of Gladys' nice cups of tea." he said, "Go and get one will you, Ollie. When you come back, try not to show it to the crowd. It may not be a good idea to let them see us drinking."

As Oliver hurried off, David relaxed.

"So much for being in charge." he muttered, "I'm acting like a real wimp."

"We're all going to feel a lot worse before this is all over." Lieutenant Riley replied, "Don't worry about it."

"Sir." a sentry called out, "Something's happening."

"Stay here." Lieutenant Riley ordered, "I'll call you if I need you."

David happily complied and even felt better when Oliver returned with his drink. Lieutenant Riley returned as he finished it.

"It looked as if a fight was starting. Now there's a guy standing just this side of the barricade waving a cloth or something. It's not a white flag though."

"Ollie, Get up to that mike. Tell him to walk to the centre of the clear space." David commanded.

"You'll have to ask for a volunteer to go out to him." Lieutenant Riley said.

"No, I'm going to talk to him." David replied.

"You can't. You need to rest."

"I need to." David exclaimed, "This is my fault. I talked the Captain into this. I can't just hide."

His senses were returning but all he felt was fear as he stepped out between two machine-gun emplacements.

Oliver relayed the message across to the crowd and the man who had been waving stepped forward. They both walked uncertainly to the centre then stood not knowing what to say.

"I've seen scenes like this in films." the man said suddenly, "I always thought they looked corny."

David frowned, "There's no working government, no one's coming to help us and what happens next depends on the water supply. I don't need some wisecracking nutter."

"Sorry. I guess it's because I'm nervous," the man said, "Is it really that bad?"

David nodded, "How are you managing for water?"

"It trickles through at the moment, the pressure's almost gone. A lot of houses are empty so we're draining down boilers and central heating systems. You're right, more people are arriving all the time and some of them are in a bad way. We can't supply them all. What do we do?"

"You'll have to try to put up some sort barrier." David said, "Like I said, we'll take in as many children as we can. Maybe you could create a safe area for the rest and some mothers."

"How?" the man asked, "No one's going to listen to me."

"OK, I'll come across but if anyone else crosses the barrier I'm turning and running."

"I don't blame you." the man chuckled, "I'm Bill, by the way. Give me a couple of minutes then come over."

The crowd was silent and remained still as David approached.

"I can't say much more than I've already said." he called out when he was standing about three metres from the barrier, "People have mentioned the Titanic so I'll try to explain it like that again. We have a lifeboat and space for some of your children. We can help you build other lifeboats but there will never be enough. According to the doctor you can live up to eight weeks without food, but no more than six days without water and you're going to be in-a-bad-way after two or three. One idea we have is to supply you with power then you can use freezers to obtain fresh water out of river water. You could try stills as well. The trick is to make it clean enough to prevent disease. If you don't all shout at once I'll try to answer any questions."

"What gives you the right to take all that food?" someone called out.

"You haven't been listening." David replied angrily, "I don't care about the food. It's water that's a problem and there's only two or three days to sort it."

"Yes but why don't you share what you've got with us."

"How many of you are there?" David asked. He stood waiting, obviously expecting a reply.

"I don't know. A few thousand. You can't let them all die."

"We reckon that we can keep a few hundred alive. There just isn't enough water."

The man was silent. David was surprised that there was no panic, no hysteria and not even any screams. He reckoned the crowd numbered thousands and could swamp the tiny group on the quay but his brutal honesty was making a deep impression. It was as if their heads understood the logic of the situation but their bodies were not yet ready to panic.

"Yes but you're OK. You'll live."

"For how long?" David asked, "I started off planning on lasting six months longer. That's when food will be a problem. We've got to plant crops and make sure they're not grabbed by loads of starving survivors. Does anyone know how to find water and dig a well?"

The part of the crowd that could hear him were thoughtful

again while the rest seemed reassured by the calm of the conversation. There was a sudden commotion to one side. Two men carrying guns clambered across the barricade dragging a battered and bruised Mr. Smith with them.

His clothes were torn, his glasses were gone and he had a deep cut to his forehead.

"You're going to do it our way or your mate gets it." one of the men yelled.

David turned to Bill.

"Someone else has been watching bad movies." he chuckled.

Bill laughed as well. It further reassured the crowd that they could be so relaxed and they waited, distracted from their fears by the unfolding drama. David turned back to the gunmen.

"If you want to tell me to freeze get it over with." David called out to the gunmen, "Feel free to kill Mr. Smith. It'll be quicker than typhus so you'll be doing him a favour."

One of the gunmen shifted his aim.

"Supposing we kill you instead." he called out

"Then you can explain to the crowd why the troops pull out without their kids."

The man's gun wavered.

A shot rang out and the man collapsed, a dark stain spreading out across his chest. There was a shocked silence. Even David stood transfixed trying to understand, but as everyone turned to him he recovered. He glanced behind him to see Lt. Riley beckoning him to return. He turned to the surviving gunman.

"Drop your weapon." he shouted, "Just get back behind the barrier before you get yourself shot as well. Bill will you help Mr. Smith over here. I'm going to break my own rule and take him for medical treatment."

"No. I still have a job to do." Mr. Smith gasped, "I'd appreciate some water though."

David turned to the crowd, "Yesterday, this man went back to you to help save your children and he wants to try again. Does anyone object if I get him fixed up first?"

David was sure that a few of the crowd shook their heads. Encouraged he added, "Bill's coming across as well. He'll be briefed on the power supply we're setting up. Like I say, use it for getting drinkable water."

They headed for the river-bus where Mr. Smith told them his story.

"There's not much to tell." he said, "People are getting pretty panicky. Locals are trying to store water while it lasts. They'll fight over a container but it's the refugees from London that are causing the real problems. They'll kill for a can of drink. Groups turn into a mob and attack a house especially if they think the occupants are hoarding water. Some haven't had a drink since they left. Some seemed to have all the drink they need."

He paused, gratefully sipping from a cup of tea, "You say that people can't last for more than six days without water. We're finding people not coping after a day. Refugees are arriving confused, delirious and just falling asleep because they think they're safe. It's terrible but no one gives them water. They're too scared of giving away their own supplies and it stays pretty quiet for the same reason. People stay at home protecting their water

"My house is in the outskirts on the London side. It was broken into by a group that was carrying backpacks full of cans. They found the radio you'd given me and I told them why I had it."

Mr. Smith was rambling, jumping from one part of his story to another, "Some refugees are pretty ill. I've heard talk of dysentery and a lot complain of chest pains and cramps. This lot were fit enough but they stole my food and reckoned that I could get them more. I'm not a strong man and I'm not used to physical violence. There's another man and a couple of women back at the house plus the two who brought me to the barricade."

"So you can't go back and you can't stay." David said, staring into space. His stomach churned at the thought of another problem.

Deep down he knew the problem but he could not face it. In a way, Mr. Smith was part of his gang and the raiders were a rival one. It was now his job to prove that he was tougher and stake his claim on Mr. Smiths supplies.

Others had gathered round to listen to Mr. Smith's story and with a start David realised that they were waiting for him to say something.

"Julia, shouldn't you go and arrest them for breaking and entering or something?" he asked as brightly as he could.

He was not serious but he needed time to think.

"With whose army?" she riposted, sensing his mood.

"That's the point, isn't it?" David answered, "It's nobody's army any more. They've as much right to it all as we have to our supplies. Ollie, go and find Commander Richards; Major Davies too. Ask them to come here, would you, please?"

Gladys stared at him thoughtfully, wondering why she felt uneasy as he asked for all the river-bus crew to stay near.

Commander Richards was obviously irritated at being sent for but as they all settled down with cups of Gladys' tea, he relaxed seeing that David obviously had something important to say.

"Sorry about dragging you all together like this." he began, "But I only wanted to say this once. I'm taking one of the work boats and heading back. There's mum to think about and there's Carol. I haven't really thought about her since all this started but I am now. I suppose I only thought of her as an occasional fu…"

He paused glancing at Gladys, "Occasional girlfriend but we did talk once about getting a flat and it felt good if you know what I mean. Anyway I want to find them and if possible bring them here."

"What about all that guff that if you leave you don't come back?" Martin, the youth that David spoke to at breakfast, exclaimed.

David nodded, "You're right. I'm more likely to get myself killed than find them. Everyone's looking at me as if I can save them and I can't do it. All I'm doing is fu… mucking around hiding behind a load of sailors and soldiers. I don't belong here."

"I agree with that young man." Commander Richards said, "You're breaking the protocols you created."

He paused, "I suppose that's the pompous way of putting it. You've made it clear who we can save and who we can't as well as how to do it. Now you want to throw it all away. I'm worried about the affect it'll have on morale if you don't believe in your own plans."

"I believe in them." David said, "I'm just not the one to rely on."

"Don't sell yourself short, lad." Tom said, "I've said before, you've got a good head on your shoulders. You see problems and plan for them. I'm sure others have said that in different ways but it's true. So far as I'm concerned you're in charge. If you think it's safe to go back, then we'll all go."

David glared angrily, "I'm not in charge. I don't want to be in charge and I don't know how to be in charge. I'm here because it seemed best for me. Now it's best for me if I go."

"OK you're not prepared for this." Tom said, "None of us are. We've all got to accept that the world has changed. I know it's been eating at you that you just left your mother but you also reckon she's got ways of looking after herself. Maybe she's a survivor, just like her son."

David smiled, "Perhaps. I still feel as if I should try though."

"Maybe the reason that we've not heard from Dover is a simple power failure." Commander Richards said, "I'm ordering another recce. If it's not operational as a regional command centre then I'm declaring Tilbury as such."

He stopped seeming to collapse again but recovered, "According to the doctor we're all liable suffer from post traumatic stress. We won't think straight and it'll be an effort to do anything."

He paused again struggling to marshal his thoughts before quietly adding, "It'll also be very difficult to forget those we're letting die. Gravesend's just across the river. We've not even considered the people there."

David nodded, "Is Gravesend bigger than Tilbury?"

Tom nodded, "It's not the problem though. There're lots of small communities that have grown and merged into built up areas. Word's going to get around and we could be swamped."

"I know I'm rambling," Commander Richards continued, "but I find it difficult to believe that the chain of command is already gone and we're not working to some sort of plan. David, it would be pointless arresting you to keep you here but I need your help. I can't force you to give it but I'd like you to stay. It's getting late so would you be prepared to stay until tomorrow?"

"We can load the boat and leave early." Ollie piped up.

"You're not coming." David snapped, startled.

"Yes I am. We'll take some shotguns and I can guard the boat for you."

"Lily said I should use my officer training." Damien said, "I'll come with you as well. All I'm doing here is looking at that crowd and wishing I could do more."

"I'm going back to my ship." Commander Richards said, "There's enough light for a recce of Dover. I don't suppose that you'd go with them would you, David?"

David wanted to be alone. He did not like having so much responsibility. He was confused. Others were following him and trusting him. He was used to looking out for himself not giving much thought to the others he had left behind because, before the flare, he would not have been expected to.

His mother would have clung onto him without thinking of his safety and he had stayed clear without seriously thinking about hers. Logically, he considered that he had done the right thing but emotionally he felt like a heel, increasingly so as he considered the support he was getting from the others.

"OK." he said, "I'll go but I want to swing up past the M25 first. You need some idea of what to expect."

"No." Commander Richards said firmly, "I need to know that the government's gone. If it is then I'll order rescue flights for our families, starting with yours. Long term, we've got to think about defensible farmland and water supplies. I'm thinking of a small island or peninsular."

"I thought that was why we were moving to Sheerness," Tom said, "but then we decided to stay here."

"It's on the Isle of Sheppey but Sheerness is still a town." Commander Richards replied, "We'd have the same problem with water and sewage. I'm talking about somewhere uninhabited or only lightly populated."

"What do you say, David?" Tom asked.

"No." Ollie snapped, "Leave him alone. He needs to rest."

Once David might have beaten Ollie up for suggesting he was weak but he remembered just in time. It woke him up enough to say, "I am tired but I'll do this trip to Dover."

He paused, "Things are confused. People are staying indoors near what's left of the water, they're out raiding the pubs and malls. Gangs from London are organised and stealing everything they can yet there are bodies everywhere where they're already dying of thirst and exposure. We're well off here and don't know what the real world's like. We've got to find out.

"I'll do what Commander Richards wants today but tomorrow we follow land routes into London to see what's really happening, check my place out then check as many other places out as we can. We just can't carry on hiding."

It seemed only moments later that David was strapped into the helicopter, nervously staring at the open door as the ship, the river and the ground dropped away. A crew member sat beside him trying to brief him on safety procedures.

"I know." David yelled, "I shouldn't be allowed on without proper training. If I get killed, then I'll sue Commander Richards."

The airman grinned, "Let me do what I can. I don't want to be court-martialled for letting it happen."

They flew at about a thousand feet but at David's request they swung round to follow the A2/M2 London-Dover road. David was surprised to see the motorway clear of traffic. Then he looked again. Tailbacks started at the approach to exits and roads leading into towns were completely gridlocked.

There were bodies along the road and in the surrounding fields. Again nearer communities, the number of corpses seemed to increase. David could not work out any pattern for the living. Some communities seemed deserted until residents stepped out of their homes to look hopefully upwards. Others were crowded with people milling about. The one thing David was sure about that there was no organisation or control.

Dover was at a standstill except for the queues. One led to the castle and everyone was holding a large container or bucket. Other queues formed to ships in the docks.

Road blocks seemed to have been set up to protect the town nearest the docks but it was incomplete and easily evaded. Armed soldiers were evident in the crowds. Near one of the gaps in the barricade David was sure he saw a firing squad. Certainly there was a pile of bodies behind a nearby wall.

No flags flew over the castle. David did not realise the significance until the airman pointed out that a flag was the badge of whoever was in control. In his own way David understood. He could not imagine some puffed up official not showing off his position.

Suddenly the helicopter made a stomach wrenching turn and climbed rapidly, disturbing his thoughts.

"They were aiming at us." the pilot informed them over the intercom, "I don't think they fired but I'm heading back."

"Agreed." David said, "Would we know if a bullet hit us?"

"We'd notice if the engine stopped. I suppose it could nick a fuel pipe without us hearing it. Why?"

"No reason." David replied, "I'm just agreeing that we should get back."

Night 5

David just wanted to be alone however he sat trying to make sense of what he saw as he talked to Commander Richards.

"My guess is that they've already abandoned Dover." he said, "If it had been stocked and just ready to open then they might have done something. Going back to the first trip and the convoy that was attacked, I reckon the locals got pissed at the idea of their food being taken up to the castle to feed a bunch of fat-cats."

"It was still mutiny and rebellion though." said Major Davies.

"We're not exactly popular here and we're trying to help." David retorted, "Take a trip into town if you don't believe me."

"I can see it from their point of view." Major Davies said, "I'm unhappy about it though because it's against my training. What about anywhere else?"

"It's confused. I'm sure most are obeying those government broadcasts and staying indoors. It makes sense as long the water lasts. As it fails they have to look for more. We flew past Faversham and there seemed to be a lot of people out and about. There's a big old brewery there that uses a lot of water. I wonder if they've got wells that are still open. It might explain how a place that size can keep going."

"But it won't last." Commander Richards said, "There's still heating and food to consider."

David nodded, "We saw a few cars and lorries moving on the motorways. They're clear. So were one or two of the exits. At others there were tailbacks a couple miles along the motorway. If a junction got blocked by drivers getting impatient or the odd accident blocked the road then the traffic just tailed back and filled all the surrounding roads."

"I was caught in a hold up once." Major Davies said, "There was an accident on a bridge. Within three hours the main roads in a fifteen mile radius were at a standstill. A half hour journey took me seven hours."

"Are you saying the Regional Command Centre has been abandoned?" Commander Richards asked, "Lieutenant Carstairs?"

"Yes sir." the pilot replied, "I can't help wondering if the officials in charge panicked and left by helicopter leaving the troops behind."

"How about transferring command to a ferry that's put to sea?" Commander Richards asked.

"It's possible but I saw no signs of a unified command, sir."

Commander Richards thought for a moment, "David, in your opinion who is the senior official in charge of the South East Command?"

"There is no South East Command." David said bluntly, "Rat's desert a sinking ship, don't they? I'd say you were now the senior rat who's staying."

Commander Richards frowned angrily then he chuckled, "I think that could have been a compliment. Just remember, when you're in front of the crew you're a senior rat as well. Major Davies, as the other senior rat do you concur that command has passed to us."

"We keep going over this." Major Davies exclaimed angrily, "We're both ignoring orders and facing court-martial but what else can we do?"

"Major," David said quietly, "We'll be going over this one more time. Tomorrow we need to check out London. If there is any government, then that's where they'll start restoring order. It won't hurt to keep looking."

Commander Richards looked at him gratefully, "Unless you have anything to add Lieutenant Carstairs then I think we've covered everything. Tomorrow we'll start reconnaissance flights over London. David, if Lieutenant Carstairs has no objections then I'd like you to go as well."

"I've no objections, sir." Lieutenant Carstairs said, "I'll prepare a flight plan."

"Why?" David asked.

Lieutenant Carstairs looked him then nodded slowly, "Some procedures might be redundant now but I'm staying safe. That means I want you at the hangar an hour before take off for basic safety training."

David nodded in his turn.

"Aye, aye sir." he replied cheekily before adding, "That's the right answer isn't it?"

"And I keelhaul mutineers." Lieutenant Carstairs grinned, "It's quite an experience at 5,000 feet."

As David laughed with him, Captain Richards coughed gently, "Gentlemen let's not forget what we're dealing with."

"I'm not forgetting." David snapped, "I just can't sit here all calm and collected all the time. Can you?"

"No, and I apologise. Get some rest and we'll see what tomorrow brings. Oh and I'll try to remember that you're a civilian."

Ollie came over though David thought he was more reluctant than usual. He had been talking to one of the girls who they had found on the quay. David grinned to himself.

At least he's not gay, he thought to himself and was less worried when Ollie threw his arms around him in one of his massive hugs.

The rest gathered around, anxious for news.

"In some places you could think everything was cool." he said as he finished, "There's no electricity though and other places look like a war zone. We saw one body hanging from a lamp post."

"Is there any sign that they're getting it under control?" Julia asked.

David shook his head, "No. Some communities may be organising themselves the way we are but we're the largest."

"You didn't land to ask anyone." Craig stated, almost accusingly.

"No." David agreed, "There wasn't time and don't forget, Julia's here because someone took pot-shots at her helicopter. If we're in the air flying over a government force then we'll find ourselves with an armed escort and a very firm invitation to land and have a chat."

"OK but what about military bases or airfields?" Tom asked.

"We didn't fly over any. Tomorrow I want to fly a little way round the M25 then head into London. Ollie, I said I'd make a daily announcement. If I'm not back in time, would you get Lt. Riley to explain what I'm doing and I'll tell them about it when I get back?"

"I could do it." Ollie said.

"I don't mind. Keep it simple and say we're looking for any sort of government that can help us."

Ollie nodded.

Not even the children could lighten the mood and soon everyone began preparing for bed.

Ollie nestled into David.

"I like Anne." he said, "How do I ask her to… you know… do stuff?"

The question threw David. It was not a question he could imagine anyone asking. Maybe it was the sort of thing a son could ask his father but since his father vanished long ago he was not sure.

With everything else on his mind the question was a distraction he did not need. It was also something of a shock to realise just how much Ollie trusted him.

David sensed that Ollie had not whispered as quietly as he should have done. There seemed to be an unnatural silence as everyone around them kept still waiting for his answer.

He thought about his first few clumsy fumblings with girls on the estate and how he talked up a simple grope into something far more than it had been but it was all different now. Ollie had been the first to look up to him and be there for him. He could not laugh at the boy for being so uncertain and shy, neither could he do the teen male thing and describe girls as either willing sluts or, if they did not willingly fall into his arms, lesbians.

David wrapped his arms round Ollie, pulling him tight in a protective hug.

"Be nice to her." David said, "But don't go any further. I doubt that she happened to be carrying contraceptives with her and you haven't got any rubbers have you? If you want to go further do it in your mind and use your right hand."

"Oh!" Ollie exclaimed a little shocked, "I bet you were younger than me when you went with a girl."

"Probably. And I don't think I thought about getting her pregnant but you're kinder than me. She's got enough to handle at the moment and you'll feel bad if she has to carry your kid."

"I'd be careful." Ollie said, "I did this stuff in sex education."

"It's up to you." David replied, "I've told you what I think. Now get some sleep."

Day 6

If Ollie and his problems had provided a little light relief then David was visibly shaken when he returned from his flight the next morning. He left Lt. Carstairs to brief Commander Richards and headed straight for the river-bus.

At first, he did not want to talk then once he started he could not stop, holding the hand of a young girl he had brought back but in the safety of the river-bus he built a picture of events.

The sudden power cut had left the barriers at the Dartford crossing toll booths down causing tailbacks in both directions, within an hour they were several miles long and increasing. Communications were disrupted by the solar flare and the operators were reluctant to raise the barriers on their own initiative so by the time they acted, the damage was done.

Initially drivers patiently waited with their vehicles until the first of the emergency broadcasts. Even then most only reacted slowly, reluctant to start walking. It was only as the first few trudged past that many began to follow. At that time of day traffic was mainly shoppers or parents on the school run. Most made it home.

As businesses began releasing employees so traffic began to build. It's often claimed that traffic flows better when a single set of traffic lights are out but when they are all out it becomes more difficult. Traffic wanting to turn right relied on oncoming vehicles to leave a gap. Some tried but began edging forward when the turning stream got too long. Drivers became frustrated trying to edge out of side turns. Pedestrians tried crossing the road by weaving through the traffic.

Bumps and shunts inevitably happened. Very few were serious but even briefly checking for damage and exchanging names and addresses took time and added to the delays.

Queues at bus stops built up and railway platforms became packed. In many places staff could see the developing chaos and elected to remain at work, planning that if necessary, they would sleep on the floor.

Further, into densely populated parts of London, so conditions became more extreme. However, what David saw to start with were on the edges. Service stations, cafés, anything that sold refreshments filled up with people.

At first, with no lighting or tills they tried to close. Later as it grew dark and temperatures dropped the remaining staff offered what help they could. As shifts changed, replacements did not arrive and those that lived nearby wanted to get home.

October can still be warm during the day while at night some places can get the first frosts of winter. Most were dressed for summer and although some women wore 'sensible shoes' to work many found themselves wearing stylish high heels that were completely unsuitable for walking distances.

Those who tried to get home on foot found themselves in increasingly dire straits. They were already tired from a day's work, apart from snacks some had not eaten all day while others, working in dry air-conditioned buildings were dehydrated.

There was nothing extreme. In normal circumstances there would be no problem but they were all on the low side of being prepared for their first night.

That night, the eerie glow of the Aurora Borealis allowed them to find their way but the strange circumstances had a disorientating effect and few appreciated how much longer it would take to walk.

As exhaustion set in so body temperatures dropped and the first fatalities occurred.

Those that stayed put, reasoned that it would be pointless trying to get home only to turn round and head back into work. Some places had gas heating and were relatively unaffected. With the population nearly double the usual night time, extra demands on services were massive when there were fewer engineers available to run the system.

The City of London became eerily quiet soon after dark. People either returned to work or were trudging determinedly home. Smaller establishments, less dependent on computerised systems, improvised to stay open and did a roaring trade.

It was the outer regions that suffered the most that night. The complete lack of a police response allowed riots, looting and general mayhem but the only deaths were through violence and not the deteriorating situation. Most people stayed at home expecting to ride out the chaos.

The following day Central London was still quiet. Gas

pressure steadily dropped as did water pressure and buildings that relied on air-conditioning became steadily more stuffy.

More people began the trek home and were in a worse state than those who left the day before. As they passed into the more residential areas so they discovered that only the gangs were organised and found themselves losing anything of value or rather, what used to be of value such as phones and money.

A healthy man should be able to walk twenty miles in a day and reach any point inside the M25 ring road from the centre within three to four hours. Add on the blocked streets, the gangs, that few had eaten properly in the previous twenty-four hours and there were long queues just to get a glass of water then the journey became a nightmare.

A few who lived close in made it but the chances of getting home dropped dramatically the further they had to go. David and the others knew nothing of this as they serenely sailed along the river and even now it was difficult to imagine.

By now gas and water pressures were obviously going to fail prompting more people to consider leaving.

Although Major Davies had not realised it he had merely tried to pen in motorists caught in the open and the first few long distance commuters determined to get home.

What David saw was the aftermath of that first phase. Wherever people had gathered seeking food or shelter there were the bodies who had been weakened by lack of food and water, then succumbing to the cold.

Now, while many people were determined to stay with their homes, others began to move. With all communications gone, no one planned it but it occurred to thousands if not millions that farms and villages might have wells or other independent water supplies.

In London, since the emergency announcements, these havens were perceived to be beyond the M25 ring road.

Those who had been trying to conserve or ration water were still becoming dehydrated. They became increasingly frightened and the shock of going from a world of instant communications to a world of none also affected their judgement. Many still automatically flicked the light switch as it got dark and even more still tried filling the kettle to make a cup of tea. These were automatic reflexes but each event added to their fear and confusion.

And now they wanted to move on. Some were thinking of the little lane they knew that meandered under a bridge carrying the motorway. Maybe they had walked it when young and knew it would only take a couple hours. Motorists also knew it as a way getting to a motorway junction beyond the hold up. Those villages were already trying to accommodate stranded drivers and passengers. They had no room for the later travellers and it made little difference for they all relied on mains water.

Some planned ahead and tried carrying enough water for the journey. A few had it stolen before they left the street where they lived. For others the additional weight slowed them down

There was no real pattern. David's group had moved fast and decisively with a clear plan. Even after nearly a week others were waiting for the government to put everything right.

David was unaware of the mechanics of the disaster. He was more aware of people waving desperately as the helicopter flew over. Early in the flight David noticed the child standing by a couple of bodies. They were huddled together under a fence marking the edge of a field.

They landed.

"I lay between Mummy and Daddy last night." the child said, "Now they're very cold and won't wake up."

"They're warm now." David said softly, "They've gone to heaven and they want us to look after you now."

They continued to fly low and saw other bodies. It seemed that parents had tried to protect children to the last because there were often youngsters, some just toddlers standing forlornly or shaking bodies as if to wake them.

The realisation that they could not help them all had a deep impact on the whole of the crew as well as David.

"Forget going further in." David sobbed "I don't think I can handle it."

Even as he described his experiences to his friends, tears filled his eyes.

"We flew low to see what was happening." he said, his emotion obvious in his voice, "People waved to us for help then chased after us as we carried on. What can we do about the children? I couldn't face flying over London, just to see more and more of it. Gladys, you've got to start rationing our water more. We've got to let more children on."

Gladys caught the hysterical edge to his voice and nodded.

"You're right, of course, David." she said, "I'm just used to putting the kettle on whenever I have visitors."

"I know and you're worried about all the water in the tanks getting infected if we keep it for too long but we've got to cut down."

"I thought it was a good idea to circulate it while we could." Tom said, "It's not Gladys' fault, it's mine."

"It's the flares fault." David exclaimed, "We all forget how things have changed."

"How many are heading for Tilbury?" Craig asked.

"It's weird." David replied, "It's pretty built up all the way into the centre of London but no one's coming this way, or at least, not many. There're estates where people can almost see us but they don't seem to know about us yet. The nearest main road is about three miles away There's people gathered around ponds between the road and us but that's all."

He shuddered, "There's a railway that runs just beyond the dock area but it's hidden by an embankment. People seem to have walked past and not seen anything. There're groups of passengers at the stations we passed. I'm sure a lot were dead."

He shuddered again, tears filling his eyes. Ollie hurried over to wrap his arms around David. A seaman arrived saying that Commander Richards would like to see him.

"Major Davies is in the sick bay." the commander said, "He's in some sort shock. You should have reported to me first but how are you? Do you need to see a medic?"

David shook his head.

"I can't seem to take it in." David replied, "I half expected to see a massive crowd like when they come out of the football but there's not. There're clusters of people. There're ponds where there're loads of people. That's good."

"I doubt it." Commander Richards replied, "There's no sanitation, no water purification and no shelter. Between the various ships, your freezing scheme and other schemes we're doing better than we thought on supplying clean water but there's still not enough. The men most closely involved with those outside are seeing a lot more confusion in them. Again it's partly a shortage of water and partly a lack of heating.

"The amazing thing is how they're cooperating with the nursery. Your Mr. Smith is working wonders. He's blocked off roads to make an outer ring. Those inside are getting just enough to drink and they pass any excess out. They even let pre-teens through to the nursery."

"How many kids are there?" David asked.

"About three hundred. We might even be able to take another hundred but we're all going on half rations."

"Surely there's more than that number of kids in the area." David exclaimed.

"Yes but it's so difficult to imagine life without communications. One family may know about us yet their neighbours have no idea. Unless someone goes around knocking on doors, how do they find out? Gravesend's just across the river. We've had a couple of boats come across but there're no crowds on the riverbank. There's a few individuals that wave to us but we ignore them."

"We're OK." David exclaimed bitterly, "Fuck the rest."

"Are you suggesting that we bring them across?" Commander Richards asked.

David crumpled his shoulders shaking as he burst into tears.

"Sorry." he managed through the tears, "I just can't handle it any more."

"None of us can, David," Commander Richards said softly, "Major Davies tried enforcing that blockade. When he left it was as if he was abandoning folk who needed his help. An orderly found him in his cabin holding his pistol. He may have been about to kill himself."

"What about you. How come you're still so with it."

"I don't know if I am. You and the Major have been much closer to it all."

There was a knock on the cabin door as Lt. Riley arrived.

"I thought that you should know. Mr. Smith is reporting that there appears to be a dozen cases of typhus and two cases of cholera. He's hoping that it could be some combination of food poisoning and fear but he's not hopeful."

"So the third one's arrived." Commander Richards muttered to himself.

"Pardon?" David said.

"The Four Horsemen Of The Apocalypse." the Commander explained though it still did not mean much to David who still looked puzzled, "It's a biblical thing. The Four Horsemen Of The Apocalypse, Pestilence, War, Famine and Death. Only War hasn't arrived."

"OK and what's A Pocket Lips?" David asked.

"Apocalypse." Commander Richards corrected, "In this context they're revealing the end of the world."

"It's not revealing much. It's happening all around us." David scoffed.

"And a poetic description isn't going to soften it. Lt. Riley, you appear to be the senior military officer for the moment. What are your intentions?"

"To carry on as we are, sir," the Lieutenant replied, "We've had a couple of desertions but the rest understand what we're doing."

"And you've no problems assuming that you're the senior level of command left in the country."

Lt. Riley was quiet for a time, "We're making best the use of the resources available. I don't think that the government, the Ministry of Defence or the Americans are going to help us now so while Major Davies is ill then I'm in charge of this community's defences. I see David as being in overall charge. If the situation improves then I can report to a senior officer but I've got to stay alive to do it."

"If we accept that this is a combined service then I still outrank you." Commander Richards said, "But I agree with most of your observations. Any comments, David?"

"Yeah, you're still thinking in the old ways. Your rank doesn't matter a shit and I get fed up with these conversations. I left my Mum to die and I haven't got the guts to try rescue her even with all your helicopters, guns and troops. Don't say I'm in charge. I'm useless."

No one tried to stop him as he stomped off to return to the river-bus.

"There's something wrong with me." he said as he took Tom to one side, "I keep bursting into tears and getting all emotional. Do you reckon I'm ill?"

"No. You're in shock." Tom replied, "I've heard about Major Davies. How's Commander Richards?"

"He keeps banging on about me being the government." David replied, "It's weird. He runs that ship so you'd think he could cope."

"He's trained to fight his ship against submarines and planes." Tom said, "Even if they had radio silence he would have had his orders and would have known what's expected of him. Now he doesn't and it's all so sudden. He's latched on the idea that you were elected by us so you're the elected government. Don't expect it to make sense to you or me because it's his way of dealing with it. You're dealing with it by letting go of your emotions."

"How do you deal with it?" David asked.

"I sit in the saloon and watch Gladys." Tom replied, "She always dreamed of having a modern kitchen and now she's got one. Back home the kettle was always filled ready for a cup of tea. Now she's got the kids making stills to distil river water."

He paused as David chuckled, "Julia sits cleaning her gun. When it's back together she offers to help Gladys or tries to sit with Jessica and talk about babies. Five minutes later she's cleaning her gun again."

"What about the rest?"

"Steve, Damien and Craig, you mean?" Tom asked, "They've taken over a corner of the quay to build bigger stills. It's dangerous because they burn petrol for fuel. Once it's up and running they pass it outside and start building another. The outsiders go looking for the parts they want so it seems like they're on the right track."

"How come I've missed all this?" David asked.

"Because you've been looking out for all of us and you're doing those flights. You're still worried about your Mum and you're holding Commander Richards and Major Davies together. However skewed their reasoning seems to be, they are trying to save as many lives as possible."

"Major Davies tried to kill himself." David retorted, "So I'm not much good at holding them together. What about me? I like cuddling up to Ollie. What sort of bloke does that make me?"

"Gladys said something about you being embarrassed about it. Don't be. He's got to deal with his mother being murdered and his whole world turned upside down. If you rejected him, he'd feel desperately lonely. So would you if Ollie wasn't here waiting for you."

David nodded, "It's still wrong for me to feel that way, isn't it?"

"Like you said about Commander Richards, people can behave oddly to deal with stress. That's your oddity. Are you still thinking about taking a boat up river?"

"I should, shouldn't I?" David asked.

"To do what?"

"Save my family."

"How? Bring them back here? Barricade themselves in your mother's flat until it's all over? Ollie's not a blood relative but he's as much family now as anyone. Will you take him with you?"

David collapsed onto back into the seat.

"You win." he whispered, "I stay. I should go and find Mr. Smith and do the broadcast I promised."

"No you sit here. I'll see if I can find Ollie." Tom said, "He can look after you for an hour or so."

David nodded, "Thanks. Would you find Martin please? He's the oldest one of kids we caught on the dock."

He arrived a few minutes later and David told him to sit down.

"Do you still want to leave?" David asked.

Martin shook his head, "No. I'm helping them build those stills. I managed to give one to Dad so you're right, I am more useful here but we're just kidding ourselves aren't we? We're not going to make a difference are we?"

"That's what I'm trying to understand. You're here because Gladys insisted." David paused, "That's not true you're here because we can't turn kids away."

David grinned as Martin's face darkened.

"Count yourself lucky that you do look young and cute." he teased, "It's given you a chance. The point is, do you plan on leaving?"

Martin shook his head again, "I feel guilty for staying but I see them when I take a still over. They're getting ill, aren't they? It'll happen to me if I leave."

"I'm going across to the barricade." David said, "If I see Mr. Smith is there a message I can pass on to your family."

"Just that I'm OK." Martin replied.

Once at the barricade, David spoke with the soldiers there.

"I'd stick to the speakers, sir." one said, "I wouldn't get too close."

"In case I catch something." David said, "I know. How are the rest?"

"They're getting very confused, sir." the soldier replied, "Your guys took a new still out to the centre of the QZ. Normally a couple would come out and collect it. A couple did try but they were staggering around and didn't seem able to pick it up."

"OK, what's the QZ?" David asked.

"Quarantine Zone." the soldier paused uncertain whether to continue, but took a deep breath and added, "You know how all those disaster movies seemed to be zombies taking over?"

David nodded.

"Well I've used glasses to look at some of them in the crowd. Their eyes seem sunken and there's something wrong with their skin. You don't suppose there's anything happening, do you?"

"No." David replied firmly, "Some are more dehydrated than others. I'll get the doctor to print a list of symptoms so you know what to expect."

"Sorry sir." the soldier said, "I guess I'm letting my imagination run away with me."

"I've learnt a new word." David said, "Lethargy. It's a symptom of dehydration. There's not much of a story if zombies just fall asleep, is there?"

"No I suppose not, sir." the soldier chuckled, "Thank you, sir."

David clambered up to microphone and switched it on.

"Raise your hands if you can hear me." He said.

He was surprised at the lack of response and how much smaller the crowd was.

"The situation is still bad." he said, "We're trying to step up the water supply so don't give up yet."

There was still little response.

On impulse, he asked, "Are there any questions?"

Still, no one moved. He gave up and clambered down, deciding to head for the warehouse holding the children. Even here the mood was subdued. The children were aged between five and ten, and David guessed that they were homesick and frightened, rather than ill. Without thinking, he entered the warehouse, heading for a group of adults standing at the far end. He was delighted to spot Mr. Smith who looked tired and haggard.

Mr. Smith managed a brief smile when he recognised David.

"I can't believe it's all happening." he said, "Thank you for what you've done."

David stared at him, puzzled.

"You've saved these children." Mr. Smith explained, "Without you, they'd be dying with the rest."

"I should be doing more." David exclaimed almost sobbing.

Mr. Smith shook his head.

"No." he replied, "It's too late. The clean water's almost gone. We were organised for a couple of days, there's your freezing idea, the stills, some even managed to boil water using car exhausts then collect the steam but it was never going to be enough."

He paused, shuddering in despair, "You spelled it out and most of us accepted that we were in for a pretty bleak time. It was wonderful how everyone cooperated but strangely, I think you gave us hope. At least you gave us the idea that we might think of something to help us and we could save the children."

He smiled, "I think the parents were the only law enforcement we had. Heaven help anyone who put the kids at risk. According to the medics we're all dehydrated now. We stretched the rationing too thin. People are giving up. They go home and we don't see them again. You'll have to excuse me. I seem to have diarrhoea. I'm hoping it's due to stress otherwise it could be the start of cholera. Just in case, I won't be offended if we don't shake hands."

"You could come back with me." David said, "I sure no one will mind."

"Thank you no." Mr. Smith replied, "There's still a semblance of control so I'll perform my duty while I can but please go before my resolve weakens."

Mr. Smith turned and hurried away leaving David to make his way back to the quay.

"Halt." someone yelled, "Take another step closer and I'll fire."

David glanced around to see what the problem was before seeing an army sergeant pointing a gun at him.

"Do you mean me?" David called back, a little annoyed but also amused. David recognised him as the sergeant who had been so aggressive on the river-bus.

"Just turn round and head back." the soldier yelled.

"It's Sergeant Grimes, isn't it?" David called, "I'm David

Robson. Send someone to fetch Lt. Riley."

"I know who you are." Sergeant Grimes called back, "You're just a civilian and this is a military operation. Get back with the other civilians."

"Fetch Lt. Riley." David snapped as forcibly as he could, glancing around to spot a soldier he recognised, "You Pte. Skinner, go and get him."

The crack of the pistol echoed around the surrounding containers and warehouse walls.

"You have ten seconds to move back and I won't warn you again."

David considered his original assessment of Sgt. Grimes and it fitted. He was not interested in what was happening and could not see beyond his orders. Never mind that David instigated them, orders were orders. David was sure that Sergeant Grimes wanted to kill him but even that had to be done by the rule book and the final warning had been properly issued. Keeping his hands clear of his body, David walked slowly backwards to the warehouse that housed the children. It was still a tense moment until a clear command rang out.

"Sergeant Grimes stand down. David Robson, you're under arrest. Put your hands on your head then step forward to surrender yourself."

Puzzled, David obeyed as Pte. Skinner hurried forward to take him by the arm.

"They've all gone mad." he muttered, "Young Ollie was hanging around and I sent him to fetch Lt. Riley. I don't know what this arrest is all about."

"Would Sgt. Grimes have lowered his weapon just because he was told to?" David asked, "Maybe he won't shoot because the army's got me."

Pte. Skinner looked happier.

"OK but stay behind me." he commanded, "Don't make yourself a target."

As they reached, Sgt. Grimes and Lt. Riley, David stood submissively with his hands behind his back as if accepting his arrest.

"He left the quay, sir." Sgt. Grimes reported, "He's not allowed back. That's standing orders."

"You acted correctly, Sergeant." Lt. Riley responded,

"However, Commander Richards wants to debrief him and I have to escort him to the frigate."

"Yes sir. You Skinner, find some handcuffs." Sergeant Grimes commanded.

"That won't be necessary Sergeant. I'd like you to begin a review of the deployment."

"Yes sir." Sergeant Grimes snapped as he saluted and hurried off.

"Sorry about that." Lt. Riley said to David, "Normally he's an excellent NCO. If we had to withdraw from the quay, I'd put him in charge of the rearguard."

"But?" David asked.

Lt. Riley glanced at Pte. Skinner and a couple of others in earshot, knowing that he should not speak badly of the sergeant in front of them.

"He's old school following his father and grandfather into the service and he's not very imaginative. He doesn't talk about what's happening and if anything he's becoming more rigid in his duties."

"He's trying to hide behind his orders, you mean." David said, "We're all behaving weirdly. I won't mention which soldier was worried about zombies."

"The thing is if I'd ordered him to just let you through, something may have snapped." Lt. Riley said, "I couldn't risk a direct confrontation, so I presented him with a sound military reason that would supersede standing orders."

David nodded, "Fair enough. It might be an idea if everyone backed off and let him rest."

Lt. Riley was surprised that a few of the soldiers seemed to give a surreptitious nod. Where David was popular, Sergeant Grimes was respected if not well liked. David had pushed to attempt rescues of their families and he was trying to save lives. More importantly he was honest about the situation so they trusted him more than their sergeant in the present situation. However, they also needed the sergeant's steadiness no matter what was happening, so it helped David's standing that he was offering to support him.

Lt. Riley escorted him to the river-bus. On impulse, he boarded a work boat and headed for the frigate.

Night 6

It was getting dark as he ferried across to the frigate but he was taken straight to the Captain's cabin.

"I was going to ask to see you anyway." Commander Richards said, "I've had a signal from Portsmouth. One of the RCCs has been designated the National Command Centre. Our RCC failed. So far as they can make out there was some sort of mutiny at Dover. The Regional Officer tried to restrict water to what he called essential staff. The troops objected because their own ration was scarcely enough to survive on, took over then began distributing it to the townspeople."

He paused and smiled, "I think you'll like this. Because of my efforts to maintain control I'm promoted to Commodore with orders to take command of the Southern Military Zone. I'm to prepare a report of my operating procedures with a view to them being adopted elsewhere."

He looked at David, "I take it that you're not impressed and think that it's a meaningless gesture."

"No, it's good news. Congratulations." David said, "It's good to think that someone reckons we're getting it right. I bet you're relieved that there's still a government."

"No I don't think that there is." Commodore Richards said, "Operations locked themselves down and put themselves on a war footing. The problem was that there was no battle plan to deal with this sort of emergency, at least on this scale. They waited on orders from whatever was left of government and at the same time they were in the same sort of shock as we were.

"They haven't been idle though. They've recalled what ships they can and sent them to other ports. It seems that they have been monitoring our signals but they're rationing power so they didn't waste energy responding."

David nodded.

"Now they want to know what you've been doing." he said.

"Portsmouth's a large city." Commodore Richards said, "And Operations are beginning to realise that they're all that's left of an organised government in the area. It's the last signal I find most worrying. They want us to prepare for transfer of command here."

"No way." David said firmly, "We don't want a load of admirals stomping around giving orders."

"I agree." Commodore Richards replied to David's surprise, "I've replied that morale and discipline are very fragile and survives because of our efforts to save as many people as possible. I've recommended that they gather as many ships as possible, fill them with supplies and as many people as they can sustain for six months and sail round. I've suggested that if they give the impression of just senior ranks arriving to a bolt hole then it would become every man for himself."

"Way to go." David said, "That's not the usual way of dealing with senior officers is it?"

"No." Commodore Richards replied, "In normal times it would cost me my ship at least."

He thought for a moment, "But it's what I've learnt from you, these are the normal times now. They're the ones still thinking in the old ways."

Before David could reply, the phone rang. Commodore Richards answered it.

"Very well." he concluded before turning to David, "My apologies but I'm also thinking in the old ways. I have a new signal and I'm going to communications to read it. Breaching security to that extent would still be a major breakdown in discipline."

"Go ahead." David smiled, "When there's time, we'll have to work out who I could sell all those secrets to."

"Er, yes." Commodore Richards said, "Luckily I'm getting used to your humour."

The commodore looked confused when he returned.

"I've got a reply to that signal." he said, "My promotion came down from the National Command Centre. It seems that the Portsmouth Operations Centre has a captain in charge. He wants to know whether my evacuation orders apply to Portsmouth, the NCC or both. What do you make of it?"

"That we get told something different every time someone speaks to us." David replied, "How many admirals were trapped in cities like London? Is this NCC doing anything or has it just collected as many prats as it can and they're standing around sticking flags in a map? Why can't we talk to this NCC direct?"

"If communications are limited then Operations filter the messages and only pass on the urgent. I'll ask for the frequencies and codes and contact them directly."

"No, on second thoughts, don't do that." David exclaimed, "You'll have to obey orders again. If they really want to talk to you, I bet they'll contact you easily enough. Why not tell this Operations place to get ready to move when they can't keep going any longer. Can they send ships to Sheerness and Grain to check them out?"

"You want me to push my orders again." Commodore Richards chuckled, "As you say, the question is, how effective is this NCC?"

David nodded, "It would be great to just hand it all over, wouldn't it."

Commodore Richards nodded, "I still won't break the chain of command if there is one. I will inform Captain Barclay that we are preparing contingency plans in case of a complete breakdown of authority and I'd like his assessment of how urgent they are."

"That's about all you can do." David said, "I'm going back to tell my lot what's happening then get some sleep."

As David stood so did Commodore Richards who put on his hat and saluted.

"Thank you David." he said, "Because of you I feel as if I'm contributing something."

David was unsure how to react. Instinctively he nodded then held out his hand.

Ollie unashamedly sat on his lap as David recounted events.

"If there is a government then I should report in." Julie said.

"Let's wait and see." David said, "I've confessed to being a car thief and escaping arrest. What are you going to do about that?"

"Point taken." Julie smiled, "It's not going back to normal is it?"

"I don't know but let's look after the kids for now."

"You've changed." Gladys said, "You've grown up so much. You get into a sleeping bag now and I'll bring you a cup of hot milk. Enjoy it because it's the last of the milk."

"That's an adult for you." Tom laughed, "Sent to bed early with a hot drink."

"I don't care." David exclaimed, "I want to forget today."

Day 7

David managed to sleep late until Commodore Richards sent for him.

"I've got a reply from Portsmouth." he said, "Here, read it."

The message was brief:- *Suggest contingency plans are completed with utmost despatch. Request that this base be designated as under Southern Military Command. Will await orders.*

"A bit terse isn't it?" David asked.

"We're using a short wave link. Data transfer is a lot slower so long messages are out."

"Is that designation request a polite way of mutinying?"

"You've got the idea." Commodore Richards chuckled, "I've passed on instructions regarding supplies and survivors."

"There's something else that we have to think about." David said, "Water long term."

"Wells and the like, you mean" Commodore Richards said, "What are you saying?"

"I don't know." David said, "We haven't thought beyond who we can keep alive. We won't be the only survivors but we might be the best organised."

"Go on." Commodore Richards prompted.

"I don't know." David said again, "Even when we were shooting our way out of London, we didn't stop anyone doing their own thing. Not even the supplies we took would have made much difference. What happens when we need to find a well and there's a group of survivors huddled around it or it doesn't supply enough for all of us?"

"And if Portsmouth joins us then the problem gets bigger." Commodore Richards said.

"Before this happened the government would tell the Navy what it wanted and then the operations base would tell you." David said, "You wouldn't contact the government direct because of this chain of command thing. If Portsmouth shuts up shop, then you'll have to deal with the NCC direct. If you tell them that we're well organised, then they'll want to come here."

Commodore Richards nodded, "We're back to whether I

should mutiny or not, aren't we?"

David also nodded.

"Why not beat them to it?" he asked, "Why not ask for their plans? You're a commodore now in charge of southern England. Surely you need to know?"

Commodore Richards nodded again.

"Good point." he said then smiled, "I believe that you compared us to a lifeboat on Titanic. I'll explain to Captain Barclay that he's got to build his own but we'll help him. We'll call all these plans 'Operation Abandon Ship' and when it's implemented it'll be everyone for themselves."

He paused and stared at David, "Abandon Ship is the last order that a captain can give. I'm still finding it difficult to accept that the ship of state has nearly gone but it's still my duty to keep it afloat if at all possible. However…"

He trailed off, uncertain how to continue. David just nodded.

A New World

Ollie sat in the stern holding the tiller as his two sons pulled steadily on the oars. David was content to sit quietly studying the river banks passing by. They had passed small communities along the river, and other boats out fishing, willing to stop and talk to a rare passing stranger.

Ollie had arranged the trip so that David could finally lay to rest the ghosts that haunted his nightmares. Ollie was thirty two now, his older son sixteen and his younger one fifteen, they were born, three and four years after the disaster. The old world that the old folk talked about was the stuff of fables and legends but they had stared in awe at the amazing bridge that they had passed under on the second day of their journey. Now they were becoming nervous as the countryside disappeared and they were surrounded by the decay and ruin of a long abandoned London.

Ollie had expected an eerie silence but birdsong filled the air; cliffs were cliffs no matter how they were formed. Underground rivers had become blocked and pushed upwards through any weakness to form ponds and streams providing myriad insect life and a whole range of small animals found food amongst the encroaching vegetation.

Ollie pointed.

"Is that the creek?" he asked, "That could be the cash-and-carry."

David nodded, "Pull over and let's have a look."

Ollie nosed the boat into the creek heading for the remains of the pontoon.

"Lucky the tide's coming in." he said, "You'll be able to climb onto the quay."

David nodded, "I'll have a scout around and then we'll decide what to do."

"You say people lived here so where are the farms?" Tom, his elder son asked, "Did those rust heaps really carry supplies all around?"

"Oh yes." Ollie replied, "Though these here were boats. But in a car, we could have travelled here in an hour or so. "

"You oldies talk about hours and minutes but why bother about them?" Ollie Jr asked.

"Nowadays, I don't know." Ollie conceded, "As long as we're up in time to work the fields it doesn't matter now, does it."

They were interrupted by David returning carrying rusting tin cans.

"It looks as if it's in good condition and there're piles of these. So much for food distribution." he said.

"There's so much mould but does it say, baked beans?" Ollie asked.

David nodded, "It's amazing how everything is so well preserved here. The roof on the warehouse is intact and someone nailed all the doors shut. The tins look OK, a bit rusty but nothing serious. The bread we brought is getting a bit dry so let's try some good old fashioned beans on toast tonight."

"Cans are an old way of preserving food." David explained to the teenagers as they settled down that evening."

They made a small fire on the wharf after carefully scraping away a circle of moss that covered the concrete. The boys cautiously tasted the beans but they lived in a time when it did not pay to waste food and they seemed to be enjoying them. Young Ollie paused just long enough to say, "You talk about escaping from here and reaching that place Tilbury but you don't talk about how you moved to our home."

"No we don't." David said, "I still get nightmares about it. Sandra gets quite worried about them. Maybe it's time I did talk about it all and lay some ghosts."

He shuddered, "All I remember of Tilbury were the bodies and an ever growing stink. Our boat holds us and supplies for a month. Now imagine, something happens, we have to abandon our community and our boat's the only way to escape. Do we fill the boat with as many people as possible knowing that they'll starve or do we take just one or two plus supplies to get us started again?"

"And that's what you had to decide." young Tom said and David nodded.

"What about here?" Ollie asked, "How come it wasn't gutted?"

"I seem to remember that they went after booze then luxury stuff." David replied, "I reckon they came back for bottled water but they'd left it too late. Someone was thinking of food though and planned on coming back but never did."

"You talk about the three horsemen don't you." Ollie Jr said, "Thirst, Cold and Disease and the fourth one, Hunger but it didn't have much to do."

"Do you remember Commodore Richards?" David asked, "He died about five years ago. He first talked about the four horsemen of the Apocalypse though I think that they were different ones. Anyway of our first three, Thirst arrived followed by Disease but it was Cold that really finished things.

"You see most people relied on heating coming through wires and pipes. So they were not only trying to find water, they were trying to keep warm. Something else we used then, petrol. They tried burning that and it was too dangerous. Sometimes they burnt down whole rows of houses. Others tried wood in containers. They sealed the room against draughts and forgot that a fire needs oxygen like them and they suffocated. It all started in October and just got colder until the snows came."

He paused, shuddering as he remembered.

"We all felt bad that we were warm and safe but what could we do?" he continued, "It all boiled down to how many we could save and it wasn't many. We struggled the next spring because nearly all of us took pity on someone and let them in. Yet we lost a lot of our original number. Some just committed suicide and others went to look for their family."

"I still don't understand why you talk about the smell." young Ollie said, "Was it that bad?"

"We left Tilbury sometime in the second week and headed round the coast to the Blackwater River." David began, "There were a couple of islands where we could winter. There was a town Maldon and someone said the population was about fifteen thousand. By the time we had sorted ourselves out and checked, we could see bodies in the streets. A couple of hundred survived the winter and the rest were just rotting away. It was the same everywhere.

"That's when we shifted to Bradwell and settled on the peninsula. We had clean water, manpower and Professor Jacobsen who really knew his stuff. It was remote, the farms at the tip had survived pretty well, provided local knowledge and gave us a good start to farming in the area. We did okay but for years, when the wind was in the wrong direction we could smell the towns.

"Despite everything we managed a good harvest that year. We had strict rationing though and I can remember always being hungry."

"So can I." Ollie said, "And I can remember teams in bio-suits heading for the towns to find extra food."

"What are bio-suits?" Tom asked.

"They were on the frigate." Ollie explained, "They were special suits that protected you from health hazards."

"Germs you mean." Tom said brightly and Ollie nodded.

"They were looking for tins like these and other stuff that may have survived."

"And the outsiders didn't mind?" Tom asked.

"That first year we could do a lot of the work in the old ways." David said, "We could also use the old stuff to look for springs and had the manpower."

"By old stuff you mean helicopters, electricity and stuff." Ollie Jr said.

"That's right." David said, "We could set up survivors with their own farms in exchange for preserved food."

"There's something I've never asked about." Ollie said, "What happened to the other ships that were supposed to be coming?"

"We don't know." David replied, "We lost contact with Portsmouth after they said that they were evacuating and we never heard from them again. That's when Commodore Richards accepted that we were on our own and we prepared to leave."

"And we're still the best organised and advanced community." Ollie Jr said proudly.

"We're the largest that we've come across and we started off by trading for what we wanted rather than fighting for it. I remember one man, Sergeant Grimes, he disagreed with us and when he went on a scavenging expedition he opened fire on some town's folk. He claimed that his orders were to secure supplies and that's what he was doing. When we said that we were taking it all back he said that we were traitors and told his men to draw their weapons."

"You shot him, didn't you?" Tom asked.

"It's one of the things I regret but I couldn't see any choice. It's sad, because being a soldier was all he knew and he refused the new reality. I made his team return the supplies that they had taken and then negotiate the way we usually did. It worked and word seemed to go ahead of us that we'd always be fair. What you call outsiders started approaching us instead of being scared of us."

"And that's why we've got schools and hospitals while others just live in mud huts." Tom said.

"The frontier's pretty wild but we're pushing out all the time."

"It all sounds pretty good to me." Ollie Jr said, "Why do you hate it?"

David was silent for a long time before finally answering, "We made mistakes and people died. We abandoned everyone we loved, we watched millions die. I lived near here and I left my mother and my girlfriend behind. I became friendly with a man at Tilbury. When I last saw him, he was dying and I couldn't save him. It's what we did to survive but it's those things that still hurt."

"Quiet." Ollie hissed, "I thought I heard something."

Carefully they drew their firearms, the last relics of the frigate.

"I see something." Tom whispered, "Over by that metal stuff behind David."

He darted off into the shadows. David thought that he caught a glimpse of him circling round in the shadows. There was a scuffle and Tom appeared dragging two children. As they got closer David could see they were naked, about ten years old, a boy and a girl. They were under-nourished and thin for Tom held their wrists with just one hand as they struggled uselessly. David wondered why they weren't yelling or screaming.

Once in the circle lit by the fire they seemed to relax, staring at the remains of the meal.

"Hungry?" David asked.

The two children stared at him and the boy nodded.

"Tom, cook some more baked beans and use up the last of the bread. It's not going to last long anyway."

It was Ollie who heard something again but this was different. They were adult voices and in the distance was the glimmer of flaming torches.

"They want us." the boy whispered sounding terrified, "We hungry. They not kind."

David guessed that the boy had missed out 'we stole food' from his explanation.

"OK let's get back on the boat." David said, "We need to do it now before the tide drops any further and we're stuck here until morning."

No one argued but they were slowed as the two children gobbled their food before climbing down onto the boat. They dropped anchor in mid stream and watched in silence as shadowy figures searched the quay and found the remains of the fire.

Briefly David could see faces clearly. Despite ragged beards they seemed much younger than Ollie and they were looking in wonder as they scraped the last of the beans from the cans. The torches flickered again and the scene was gone but he was sure that the leader was glancing from the can to the warehouse in some sort of understanding.

While Ollie and his sons kept watch, David fell into a deep sleep with the two children cuddled up to him. For once, he was untroubled by nightmares for he had done what he had needed to do. He had rescued people from his home and had at last, seen, that the food in the warehouse was properly distributed.

Notes For Fracture Point

Appendix A

The next time your bank card is replaced, don't cut the old one with scissors. Instead, bend it to and fro until you see a white line appear. The card's fracture point has been reached and it is now irreparably damaged. Continue to bend it to and fro and eventually it'll split in two. The question in this tale is, how easily can civilisation reach its fracture point before disintegrating and throwing us back into the stone age?

What we tend to forget is that the basic rules of survival still exist even if they are all wrapped up in modern comforts so consider the survival rule of three. We can survive,
- 3 minutes without air,
- 3 hours without a regulated body temperature (shelter),
- 3 days without water,
- 3 weeks without food.

Now let's think about what would happen if the electrical supply was disrupted? You'd think that it wouldn't affect the air so we'd have more than three minutes but what about skyscrapers and high rise office blocks? They rely on air conditioning. Emergency generators would kick in but for how long? If buildings running essential services became uninhabitable what would happen?

Imagine that it is October and you are contemplating the onset of winter with neither central heating, nor electric or gas fires. Plenty of warm clothing and huddling together would help but the elderly and the disabled would be affected almost at once, even in October.

Although there would be tragic consequences, civilisation could probably survive the shortest two deadlines but what about the third? More than anything we take water for granted. We have a modern, efficient supply that rarely fails. But what if the computers controlling it failed? What if engineers could not be contacted, let alone get to a repair, and what if the water processing units failed disrupting supplies at source?

Maybe events would proceed more slowly than I depicted in

Fracture Point but more than any other utility the water supplies would have to be maintained from day one. The water companies will tell you that they have stocks of emergency fuel and could keep going.

The problem is that they're dependent on other services. Try sending a repair team to a burst pipe, for a start. Vans and lorries need fuel. Would petrol stations be operating albeit far more slowly as the pumps were hand cranked or would staff be unable to get in because of their own problems? How would it be paid for without cards or credit. What problems would fuel companies have distributing it to outlets. Assuming fuel was available what would the roads be like without traffic signals, lighting and so on.

Consider the emergency backups that we're told about. How many would prove to be ineffective and how long would they last? Is maintenance never neglected? Are they all tested and maintained regularly? The water utilities are dependent on communications, which in turn, relies on power. What happens if all three suffer damage?

The answer should be that it's all idle speculation because we couldn't lose our utilities so completely, could we?

In 1859 a solar flare struck the Earth providing spectacular displays of the Aurora Borealis as far south as the Caribbean. Not only the most powerful flare ever observed, it was the first one to be recognised. It was reported by British astronomer Richard Carrington and independently by an observer named Richard Hodgson. The event is named the Solar Storm of 1859, or the "Carrington event". Although the newly established telegraph service was badly damaged, few noticed. If a farmer was working his field he might have stopped and stared as electrical sparks crackled along telegraph wires but it would be a few moments' entertainment before he continued with his work. Not even businesses in the biggest commercial centres were affected. Ships still sailed, trains still left on time and the post was still delivered.

It was a different story when a much weaker flare struck in 1989. There were no spectacular displays of Northern Lights but a power spike blew transformers in the Canadian power grid. Six million people were without power for nine hours.

These incidents pose vital questions. Was the Carrington Event the worst that the sun can throw at us? What happens if it isn't? How often do they happen?

There are all sorts of variables that could affect events, primarily, the intensity of the flare. Power cables running for miles would almost certainly induce power spikes to blow equipment connected to it. Not only power cables. What about the power lines of electric trains? The digital age relies on computers. They don't have to be damaged. Sensitive chips just need the odd molecule to be affected to create an error. It happens all the time but how many computers might need a reboot at the same time, before the system they're running breaks down.

The electrical industry is aware of the risks from solar flares and tries to make their systems safe. However, the one lesson we've learned from the Titanic disaster, through the devastation to New Orleans caused by hurricane Katrina, to the 2011 earthquake in Japan, human endeavours are easily overwhelmed by nature. In the case of the sun we are still learning about its power and strength. Another Carrington event will happen, maybe it will be even more powerful and it will test our defences.

With our dependence on electronics, could it push civilisation to its fracture point?

Appendix B

BBC transcript to be used in the wake of a nuclear attack

This is the Wartime Broadcasting Service. This country has been attacked with nuclear weapons. Communications have been severely disrupted, and the number of casualties and the extent of the damage are not yet known. We shall bring you further information as soon as possible. Meanwhile, stay tuned to this wavelength, stay calm and stay in your own homes.

Remember there is nothing to be gained by trying to get away. By leaving your homes you could be exposing yourselves to greater danger. If you leave, you may find yourself without food, without water, without accommodation and without protection. Radioactive fall-out, which follows a nuclear explosion, is many times more dangerous if you are directly exposed to it in the open. Roofs and walls offer substantial protection. The safest place is indoors.

Make sure gas and other fuel supplies are turned off and that all fires are extinguished. If mains water is available, this can be used for fire-fighting. You should also refill all your containers for drinking water after the fires have been put out, because the mains water supply may not be available for very long.

Water must not be used for flushing lavatories: until you are told that lavatories may be used again, other toilet arrangements must be made. Use your water only for essential drinking and cooking purposes. Water means life. Don't waste it.

Make your food stocks last: ration your supply, because it may have to last for fourteen days or more. If you have fresh food in the house, use this first to avoid wasting it: food in tins will keep.

If you live in an area where a fall-out warning has been given, stay in your fall-out room until you are told it is safe to come out. When the immediate danger has passed, the sirens will sound a steady note. The 'all clear' message will also be given on this wavelength. If you leave the fall-out room to go to the lavatory or replenish food or water supplies, do not remain outside the room for a minute longer than is necessary.

Do not, in any circumstances, go outside the house. Radioactive fall-out can kill. You cannot see it or feel it, but it is there. If you go outside, you will bring danger to your family and you may die. Stay in your fall-out room until you are told it is safe to come out or you hear the 'all clear' on the sirens.

Here are the main points again:

Stay in your own homes, and if you live in an area where a fall-out warning has been given stay in your fall-out room, until you are told it is safe to come out. The message that the immediate danger has passed will be given by the sirens and repeated on this wavelength. Make sure that the gas and all fuel supplies are turned off and that all fires are extinguished.

Water must be rationed, and used only for essential drinking and cooking purposes. It must not be used for flushing lavatories. Ration your food supply: it may have to last for fourteen days or more.

We shall repeat this broadcast in two hours' time. Stay tuned to this wavelength, but switch your radios off now to save your batteries until we come on the air again. That is the end of this broadcast.

Science Fiction
By
Peter Apps

The Stuart Johnson Chronicles

The Long Way Round
Time Askew
Deja Vu To The Nth
Earth Against Earth.

Short Stories

Disastrous Science

~~~

Non Science Fiction

Contributions to
Quirky Humans And Others
(An anthology by the
Sheppey Writers Group)

Peter Apps

Peter Apps lives in England, and The Long Way Round was his first novel to be followed by Time Askew and Deja Vu To The Nth. For a complete list, please visit his website at sjtales.uk

He was born in 1948 and has lived in Sheerness, Kent for most of his life. The Isle of Sheppey where Sheerness is situated has a long, rich history has always fascinated Peter. History might seem a far cry from Science Fiction but imagining life in a Roman settlement imagines a world just as alien as a distant planet.

Although he worked in a series of routine jobs, he likes to do his own thing when he can. For example, all his computers are Microsoft free zones and prefers to use Linux. He has always had an interest in science, especially Astronomy. Now that planets have been discovered around other suns, he feels that the time is coming when we could discover intelligent life out there.

Other interests include classical music and jazz. He also likes to settle down in the evening watching a good film and enjoying a nice glass of bitter and occasionally visit his local for a chat over a friendly drink.

The author is just a click away by email, peter@sjtales.uk.